DEADL

A Doris

N.C. Lewis

CW00469356

Copyright © 2019 by N.C. Lewis

This is a work of fiction. The characters, organizations, and events portrayed in this novel are the product of the author's imagination or are used fictitiously, and any resemblance to actual persons, living or dead, businesses, companies or events, or locales is entirely coincidental.

All rights reserved. No part of this publication may be reproduced, distributed, or transmitted in any form or by any means, including photocopying, recording, or other electronic or mechanical methods, without the prior written permission of the author, except with brief quotations embodied in critical reviews and certain other noncommercial uses permitted by copyright law.

DORIS CUDLOW MYSTERIES

The Doris Cudlow mysteries are set in an English seaside town, and can be enjoyed in any order.

Deadly Chapel

Deadly Sayings

Deadly Ashes

Deadly Vestige

About the town of Skegness

Skegness is a seaside town on the east coast of England, about one hundred and fifty miles from London. It is famous for its beach, offshore wind turbines...and enormous seagulls.

Chapter 1

I HADN'T PLANNED ON attending the wedding of Toby Cudlow. We hadn't spoken since the divorce. That was five years ago.

Toby's text popped up on my phone as I lay in bed scrolling through emails, a simple message, only five lines:

Doris,

Getting hooked again. Her name is Norah Porlock, lovely gal.

April 7th is the big day.

Your invitation is in the post.

LOL—Toby

This morning I could barely drag myself out of bed having slept little, my stomach tight and sour. I kept my married name, Cudlow; it made life easier, and I suppose somewhere in the back of my mind I still had hope. Now there would be another Mrs Cudlow. If I'd had the choice, I'd have stayed in bed till noon, sulking. Not today, though, the second day in a new job—full-time news reporter for the *Skegness Telegraph*. I was late on my first day.

My eyes drifted to the alarm clock—seven thirty. I didn't have to be at the office until nine thirty.

We'd met at university in London, married after graduation, and busied ourselves with our careers. Toby worked for an accounting firm. I focused on my writing. After ten years we parted on amicable terms—no children. "The divorce is only a bit of paper mumbled over by a magistrate. We'll always be friends," Toby had said on the steps of the court. I agreed but cried myself to sleep that night.

The alarm went off—seven forty-five. Plenty of time.

I pressed snooze, closed my eyes, scrunching them tight, seeing Toby's boyish good looks. He'd risen through the ranks of Stuffles and Sigley, a prestigious London accountancy firm. I'd suffered rejection after rejection for my novels, short stories and ended up a jobbing writer. Not as glamorous as it sounds: think of the instruction manual for your mobile phone or freelance articles about dull stuff mixed with long periods of unemployment.

On the steps outside the court was the last time I had seen Toby. "Promise to call me," he had said.

"Promise," I said, but never did.

Again, the alarm buzzed—seven fifty. "Ten more minutes," I said to the empty room, hand dabbing at the clock and thinking about Norah Porlock. She was probably some young nymph Toby had snatched up from college. I'd not see forty again.

"No," I said with determination. "Friends or not, I won't attend the knot-tying ceremony between Toby and the youthful, gorgeous, and no doubt dazzling conversationalist, Norah Porlock."

Anyway, I had little choice. After five years of post-marriage struggle, flat broke with credit card debts the size of

Mount Everest, I'd left the capital city for the seaside town of Skegness. The job as reporter at the *Telegraph* pays about as much as a doughnut fryer at Fantasy Gardens amusement centre on the promenade, but at least I'm a journalist. Unfortunately, I'm behind with the rent and couldn't afford a train ticket to London, even if I wanted to attend Toby's big day. A Tuesday evening acting class at the local community centre is the highlight of my week. If the lessons weren't provided free by the council, my social life would be non-existent.

The good news is the cost of living is much lower on the coast. On my first day in town, I realized why—nasty weather, vicious seas, and massive seagulls pooping everywhere. They've made a mess of my twenty-year-old Nissan Micra's paintwork. It's a little beat-up banger. The mechanic had said, "Don't worry about the spots of rust or seagull doings; you're getting one of man's finest machines. Run forever, do them Micras. Sellin' it for a song, but you gotta change the starter motor and alternator soonish."

I'd rather catch the bus, but out here buses arrive at random times, infrequently, and the drivers take great pleasure in zooming by the designated bus stops grinning. This loathsome practice seems to heighten whenever there is rain. Walking is out of the question—the seagulls.

"Broke is no joke," I muttered, pulling the covers over my head, thinking about Toby's text message with a pang of something I refused to recognize as jealousy.

I lay with my dreary thoughts for a while, then cheered up. At least with the new job at the *Skegness Telegraph*, I'd soon have a little cash. Maybe even celebrate my first pay cheque by taking the Micra to the car wash.

My eyes closed, and I slipped into a pleasant dream about seagulls, wedding cakes, and five pound notes falling like autumn leaves from a clear blue sky. Then I saw them. A grubby band of seagulls squawking and flapping their filthy wings. They waddled greedily towards the wedding cake. Another band with sticks between their beaks chased off a woman dressed in white whose face I couldn't see. Then they rounded on a tuxedo-clad man, the spitting image of Toby. For a moment longer, lulled by the warm glow of the dream, I floated on a cloud of five-pound notes.

My eyelids lifted slowly, and the alarm clock came into focus—eight fifty-five.

"Oh bugger!"

Chapter 2

I SAT UP WITH A JOLT and hoped Mr Paddington, the executive editor, would be as pleasant as he had been yesterday when I stumbled into the office late and full of apologies.

"Not to worry about a little tardiness," he had said in a clipped accent, seated at his desk in a scruffy little office. "First day and all that. Quite understandable given the circumstances. Like to get in around noon, myself. Not much happens before lunch around here. Leave at teatime." He was a plump man with a smooth blob of a face, soft-brown Bambi eyes and a ready, welcoming smile. "The name's Ian."

"Only been in town a month, from London," I explained, staring at the photograph frame on his desk. It had golden, swirly leaves and held a picture of a dark-haired woman in a blue summer smock. Probably, his wife, I thought. Then struck by a pang of jealousy at his happy marriage added, "I'm still finding my way around, looking to make new friends."

Mr Paddington nodded as if he understood. "Skegness is a hassle-free seaside town. Keep a bag of sausage rolls on hand at all times in case you cross paths with the police... You'll find the people friendly... Go on first-name terms... I insist you call me Ian... Been at the newspaper thirty-five years... They'll have to carry me out... Small newspaper, this... Owner never shows up...like living on Easy Street... Everyone calls me Ian... How are you settling into town life?... I don't know what it is, but police officers go mad for 'em... Did I say my name is Ian? Wonderful living here at the seaside... Nasty weather though. Monstrous seagulls too... Carry an umbrella...but affordable living... I insist you call me Ian."

It came as a big relief to be on first-name terms with the boss on day one. Only later did I discover "Ian" is his middle name. His first name is Rupert.

I rolled out of bed, stumbled across the room on tiptoes and covered my ears with my hands.

Thud. Thud. Thud.

"Sorry, Mr Pandy," I yelled at the floorboards. "Got a job now."

Thud. Thud. Thud.

"I've got to go to work!"

I rent a top floor room in the Whispering Towers Boarding House. Mr Pandy rents the room below. They did the conversion of the creaky Victorian mansion into bedsit apartments on the cheap. The walls are paper thin, the floorboards squeak, and Mr Pandy has enormous ears, oversized mud-brown, bloodshot eyes and a National Health Service walking stick.

Thud. Thud. Thud.

Then there is the large gap in the floorboard. One day, when I've got the cash, I'll cover it with a rug. I'm sure I've seen an eyeball peeking through—mud brown and bloodshot.

Thud. Thud. Thud.

"Shut up!" I swear the man lies in wait with his walking stick in hand. He's so finicky he'd rap on his ceiling if a mouse ran across the floorboards.

A shower has a way of invigorating the mind, releasing trapped thoughts. While the steamy, hot water splashed, I remembered what Ian had said as I left the newspaper.

"Early morning meeting Thursday. Big news. Need everyone in by twenty past nine."

Today was Thursday.

I ran from the shower, naked, leapt over the crack in the floorboard and blinked at the alarm clock—seven minutes past nine.

Three minutes to slip into a blouse and jeans; five seconds to grab a breakfast cereal bar, then I was out of the door.

For several seconds I stood on the landing blinking as my eyes adjusted to the gloom, and nose twitched at the vaguely damp, musty air.

"Yoo hoo! Doris, I thought it was you," called the landlady, Mrs Lintott, trotting up the narrow stairs.

Oh no! Not this morning, I thought, but said, "Hello, Mrs Lintott. I'm in rather a hurry for work."

"The newspaper can wait a moment or two, can't it?"

"Of course." Upsetting your landlady is a bad move, especially when you are behind with your rent. "If it is quick."

"Mr Felix has gone walkies again. Have you seen him?"

Mr Felix was her oversized cat. He was always going missing. "Have you tried the dormer?"

"Would you be a dear, and pop up and check? It won't take a moment, and what with my old legs..."

"Delighted," I said, lips curving into a smile that didn't extend to my eyes.

The dormer was a small attic-type room at the top of the building. In the old days it was rented, but nowadays served as a storage room. Like an energetic kangaroo I skipped up the stairs, pausing for a moment outside the dormer door to catch my breath—I'm not as fit as I'd like to believe.

The door to the dormer swung open after a gentle tug. "Mr Felix, come here, kitty," I said, stepping into the room. There was a slight scuffle.

Meow. Meow.

I waited for several moments hoping he would wander towards me. But not today. I'd have to get him. Huffing, I weaved around boxes, cartons, and bits of old furniture, then turned a corner that led to a disused camp bed and a little desk. Mr Felix glanced at me from the bed.

I swept him up into my arms before he could protest and headed back to the stairs. He was purring when I handed him over to Mrs Lintott.

"I knew he was up there. Naughty cat!" She wagged her finger at Mr Felix.

"Got to go now," I said.

Mrs Lintott shooed the cat down the stairs and stretched out a plump hand to lean against the banister. "Gary, the postie, came early today. "

The postman, known by all as the postie, is a weasel-faced man with a dirty smudge of stubble smeared across his chin, twitching nose, and garlic breath. He always delivers the mail early. The rest of the day he spends in Bet Quick Bookies on Ida Road.

"This is for you." Mrs Lintott held out a golden envelope with fancy calligraphic writing. "To Mrs Doris Cudlow." Her eyes narrowed. "I wonder what it is?"

"Probably junk mail," I replied, already knowing it had to be from Toby. "Give it here. I'll toss it in the dustbin on my way out." What I really wanted was to slip down the stairs, forget about the envelope and Toby.

"Not so fast!" She raised her right hand and clutched the envelope close to her ample bosom with her left. "It came special delivery. The postie doesn't get many of these."

"Everyday occurrence in London," I said with a nonchalant wave of the hand.

Her eyebrows went up. "Not round here. Special deliveries are a rarity at the Whispering Towers Boarding House, a sign we are moving up in the world."

"Oh yes," I agreed, hoping she wouldn't bring up my over-due rent. "This place is...an institution."

Mrs Lintott leaned forward and dropped her voice. "The postie said they are taking bets at the depot."

"On what?"

"The contents of this here envelope." She waved the enve-lope in the air.

"What!" I said, indignant. "The man's got a serious gam-bling problem. How he remains in the employ of the Royal Mail is beyond me. They'll hire anyone since the government sold it off."

Mrs Lintott let out a chuckle. "Mr Singh, from the post of-fice has a fiver on it being an invitation from the Queen, on account of your writing, but the postie reckons it's the golden ticket from the Skegness Players production of *Charlie and the Chocolate Factory*. I've got ten pounds on a wedding invitation."

"Give it to me," I said, snatching at the envelope and missing.

"Not so fast. Rector Beasley asked if the winner would donate part of their betting cash pool to the church reconstruction fund. It's all for a good cause."

"I'll be late for work," I said acidly. "This is my first week. I can't afford to be late."

"Weren't you late yesterday?"

"Give it here!" I persisted, snatching again and missing.

"No need to get your knickers in a twist." She handed over the envelope. "There you go, darling."

I slipped the glittering envelope into my handbag. After I'd torn it into a thousand shreds and set it alight, I planned to dump the ashes in the dustbin.

Mrs Lintott expanded her considerable girth to block the stairway. "Open it, now," she commanded. "I've got money riding on this... I have to report the contents to the postie and collect the donation for the rector."

There was a brisk finality in her tone, and I knew there was little point arguing. I tore open the envelope. My stomach did little somersaults as I pulled out the gilt-edged card.

"Surprise, surprise," I said, holding up the neatly printed card and squinting at the text: *Doris Cudlow and guest are cordially invited to the marriage ceremony of Toby Cudlow and Norah Porlock on Saturday, 7th April.* So, Toby really was getting remarried. At least I wouldn't be part of the dratted event.

Mrs Lintott's eyes glittered. "I'm ten quid up!" Then she lowered her voice. "Please tell no one about the contents. The postie likes that privilege."

"Okay," I said, letting out a mournful sigh. "Now, Mrs Lintott, I must get on my way."

"Yes, dear," Mrs Lintott said, then added, "Who is Toby Cudlow? Is he your brother?"

I mumbled an answer, but she wasn't listening.

Her eyes were half closed as if in deep thought. "The seventh is this Saturday. I've always fancied travelling to London for a glitterin' wedding."

"I'm not sure it's in London," I said. "It says the venue is the Hidden Caves Chapel on Seaview Road. The name sounds familiar."

"That's on the north side of town," exclaimed Mrs Lintott, squealing and clapping her hands together like a well-fed seal at the zoo. "I've never been to the Hidden Caves Chapel; they say it is a sight to behold. I'm coming with you."

"What?"

"Who else are you going to take? It'd be a shame to let a free nosh-up meal go to waste. Wait till I tell the ladies at the bingo club!"

Chapter 3

I GLANCED AT THE SKY. Dark clouds scudded and bunched together in a towering swirl like a crowd steam from a kettle. The Micra looked dilapidated in the dull morning light. It needed to be with its brethren in the junkyard. The first spots of rain fell on my jacket as I climbed inside.

I slipped the seat belt around me, gazed again at the sky and flipped on the radio. Blasts of wind tended to throw the car around; I wanted to know if there'd be any sudden gusts. The radio crackled to life:

It's a thundery Thursday morning. Expect intermittent showers throughout the rush hour, easing by the afternoon to a steady drizzle. Now, the Skegness FM 87.7 morning traffic report. A crash has blocked both lanes of Lumley Road. Police advise motorists to use the Grande Parade instead.

Great, I thought. That'll add another ten minutes to my commute. A flash of lightning streaked across the sky, followed by a massive roll of thunder. The rain began in earnest, clattering down on the rusted metal roof and splashing hard against the rickety windows. I flipped the ignition key. The wipers came on with a jerk, and the engine shuddered but didn't turn over.

I turned the key again.

Silence.

I tried again.

Nothing.

I closed my eyes. A black-smudged face came into my mind's eye: the mechanic. "You gotta change the starter motor and alternator soonish."

"Yes," I had said. "I'll see to it." But hadn't.

The pounding rain drummed on the windscreen as I considered my options. Option one: call Ian and let him know I will be late.

"Nope." Better to sneak in late and hope for the best.

Option two: Walk to the bus stop. That'd mean standing under a rickety shelter hoping a bus would stop. "Nope, " I said again, imagining the grinning face of the bus driver as he sped by my outstretched hand.

I called the mechanic, left a message, then scrolled through my mobile phone contacts and dialled.

"Harry Sutton Town-Wide Minicabs. Where you go, we flow," said a bored-sounding female voice.

"I'm at the Whispering Towers Boarding House and need a cab to take me to the *Skegness Telegraph* building," I said in an urgent voice.

"You are at Whispering Towers Boarding House and want to go to the *Telegraph* building. Is that correct?"

"Yes."

"We can help with that."

I sighed with relief. "Good. I'm running late and need to get to work."

"Oh, you must be Doris Cudlow."

"Yes."

"How is Mrs Lintott?"

"Very well."

The voice dropped to a whisper. "I have twenty quid on the contents of that golden envelope of yours. Tell me, did it contain a British Airways, all-expenses-paid ticket to New York? I've always wanted to visit America."

Toby always said I didn't have much of a temper, but now I was ready to snap. We'd lived in the same apartment in London for almost ten years, never knew our neighbours. Now, in Skegness everyone knew my business and were even taking bets on it.

After a deep yoga breath, I said, "I couldn't say. The postie will make an announcement. I'm in rather a hurry."

"I see," she said, in a huff. "How soon do you need our service?"

"Now."

I heard a low whistle. "Now?"

"Yes."

"No can do."

"Pardon?"

"All our cars are on the other side of town."

"Eh?"

"It's Thursday," the woman said as if that explained everything.

"Thursday?"

"The rector rides out to the Golden Shores Elderly Home, and Mrs Symons heads over to Wainfleet Cottages; she's the cleaner." She paused for a moment, then continued. "On Tuesday evening, the rector gets another ride out to the old people's home. Thursdays and Tuesdays are regular as clockwork around here."

"How many cars do you have?"

"Two."

Somehow that answer didn't surprise me. "My car's broken down," I said in a slow voice. "I need to get to work!"

"You could always get the bus."

The rain drummed hard on the car roof. "How soon can you get a cab over here?"

There was a long pause. "Listen, I can have a car out to you in forty-five minutes."

I let out an exasperated breath. "Can't you get one here any sooner?"

"I'm pushing it as it is. Antoni, the rector's driver, likes to stop and chat with one or two of the residents, have a cup of tea and a bacon roll, before taking the scenic route back into town."

"Maybe he could breakfast in town today?" I suggested helpfully.

"It doesn't do to break Antoni's routine. He grew up in Communist Poland—likes routine. Forty-five minutes is the soonest." She lowered her voice. "Ian is easy-going. He won't mind if you arrive late at the newspaper. Tell him your car broke down. He'll understand. A wonderful man is Ian."

I thanked her for the suggestion and hung up and waited. Somewhere, I can't recall the exact source, I'd read that smiling improves the mood and clarifies the mind. I tried to smile but failed.

The sky darkened further; now the rain pelted down so hard it was like a heavy blanket of fog rocking and shaking the little car.

The mobile phone rang.

"The mechanic!" I said with a frustrated sigh, picking it up without glancing at the screen.

"Doris, that you?"

I took the phone from my ear, stared hard at the screen, my mouth instantly dry.

"Doris, are you there? It's me, Toby."

For a moment I froze every muscle. "Toby?" I asked, making sure I hadn't imagined his voice.

"You remember me, don't you?"

"Toby!" I wanted to hang up and crawl back to bed. I did neither.

"Is now a good time to talk?" He sounded the same, cheerful, just as I remembered him.

"I've got nothing else to do. The car broke down."

"Are you safe?"

"Yes, help is on the way, but I fear it might be the end for my car."

"Oh dear, you on the motorway? What's that noise?"

"It's raining."

"Sounds like the echo in a cave. That reminds me, did you get the invitation?"

"Yes." I wanted to say more but didn't know what.

"Norah is from Cumberworth, just down the road from Skegness. She thought it would be nice to get married by the seaside; I quite like the idea." His voice sweetened to a low, husky tone. "Please say you'll come."

Are you crazy? I thought. "Yes, and I'm bringing a friend."

"Good. How is the journalism going?"

"Got a job as a reporter for the *Skegness Telegraph*."

"Wonderful." The line went quiet for several seconds. "Listen, my Norah is a lovely gal. I'm sure you two will get on like a house on fire. It's just..." His voice trailed off.

"Go on," I said, pressing the phone hard to my ear, and hoping he'd say he'd changed his mind about the wedding.

"She's having a bit of bother."

"What type of bother?"

"With an ex-boyfriend...a chap by the name of Leo Warrington. He's in manual work." Toby said the last two words as if they had a foul taste. "I'm convinced he's connected with the underworld. Talks like a criminal, looks like a gangster, and smokes roll-ups. I wonder if you might use your journalism skills to do a little digging. The man won't leave my Norah alone."

"Digging?"

"Just the communal garden variety. See if you can find anything down in the roots."

"Like what?"

"Oh, I don't know; maybe a little nugget I can toss to the local constabulary."

I sighed and shrugged. "I don't know. The Chartered Institute of Journalists holds reporters to high ethical standards. We can't go digging into people's backgrounds especially if they aren't a public figure."

Toby's voice rose an octave. He sounded scared. "Doris. Maybe this is a silly thing to say, but I have a feeling Leo might do something violent. I need your help. Please."

He paused, and I knew he knew I would agree. There was nothing Toby couldn't ask of me. "Sure," I said, regretting the words even as they tumbled out of my mouth. "Is Leo invited to the wedding?"

"Of course! We have invited all the ex's. Norah and I have agreed to be open about our past romances." Again, he lowered his voice. "She has rather a lot of former admirers. When you see her, you'll understand. I have to go now; can you call me this evening, and we can discuss?"

"Okay," I said reluctantly. "If you are sure."

"I am. Doris, promise you'll call me."

"Promise," I said, hand shaking. "I'll call you."

Chapter 4

AT TEN MINUTES PAST ten, I jumped out of the minicab and hurried into the *Skegness Telegraph's* headquarters. To call it a headquarters is to give it a grandeur beyond its status. It occupies a portion of a dingy warehouse with commanding views of the local supermarket and petrol station.

The newspaper's portion of the building, fitted out with tiny cubicles, contains many original features, all dilapidated, which combined with the peeling plaster, smell of damp, and only the basic amenities gives the place a spartan aura. Not that I'm complaining. It's a job, the first rung on the ladder back to respectability and more important, I need the money.

Best to have an excuse ready for my late arrival I thought, glancing up at the black clouds. Might not have to use it, but better prepared than not. I finally settled on a mixture of the rain and the breakdown of my twenty-year-old Nissan.

"Doris, you're gonna be late for the meetin'," Fred, the security guard, said with a broad grin. Then he added, "Can't see why they gave you the job. I was next in line for Easy Street. Don't suppose you know my elementary school essay came top of the class? I got a commendation from the headmaster."

I knew all about Fred's essay, and his longing to be a reporter. According to him I showed up the very moment the job was in his hands. I was the only other candidate. I gave a resigned sigh. "Press the buzzer so I can get into the newsroom, Fred. I'm running late."

He folded his arms. Today he was going to take his own sweet time. "I feel like a starved man taken to a banquet and ordered not to eat."

I rolled my eyes to the ceiling. "Press the buzzer."

"How would you feel if the bread was snatched from your mouth?" he continued to grumble. "Seven years! That's how long I've sat here!"

All the while he was talking, he was grinning. It reminded me of a cat playing with a mouse.

"Press the buzzer!" I was almost shouting now.

Fred's fleshy lips curled into a catlike smirk. "If it makes you feel any better," he said, pressing the buzzer to open the door, "Ian showed up late, made an excuse about his car breaking down and the foul weather, but she didn't buy it."

I gave an acknowledging nod and hurried into the newsroom. Big mistake. If I'd have stopped to ask what Fred meant by "she" the next few minutes would have been less traumatic. Traumatic, yes, but less so.

The newsroom was empty. A low murmur of voices carried from Ian's office. Even straining over the tops of the cubicles I could tell the entire team of fifteen had already gathered. The only exception was Fred, who darted in front and slipped into Ian's office a second or two ahead of me.

"Doris is here," he yelled like a rooster announcing the dawn. "Everyone's accounted for now, ma'am." He faced Ian's desk as he spoke and made a sort of bow.

Ian stood at the side of his desk, shoulders hunched over into a question mark. His head drooped, and the large, brown eyes seemed open too wide. They stared at the woman sitting at his desk. The woman Fred had addressed as "ma'am."

"Close the door," the fifty-something woman barked. She was a skinny twig of a thing with a brick-red face, a series of ugly scars on her left cheek and wisps of black hair growing from her chin. The dark blue business suit added to her menace. Her narrow, stone-grey eyes didn't look friendly. "Now, let's begin. Mr Paddington, you first."

"It's Ian around here," he whispered.

"Really?" Her eyes shrunk to grey dots. "Please continue, Mr Paddington."

Ian cleared his throat, shuffled forward a step or two. "Fellow journalists, I wanted—"

"Keep it short," the woman interrupted, drumming her fingers on Ian's desk.

Ian crimsoned, fumbled for words. "Yes... err... We are here today for an important..."

The woman raised her hand. "I'll take it from here, Mr Paddington."

"Yes, err..."

"Shut up, Paddington!" The woman's red face deepened, her mouth little more than a straight line, her flinty eyes were hard. "My name is Lucy Baxter. I'm in charge now. That is all you lot need to know."

There was a stunned silence. I slipped my hand into my bag ready to pull out my mobile phone and dial the police. Mrs Hairy Chin was crazy. But what the woman said next stopped me in my tracks.

"Porcherie Media Corporation concluded their purchase of the *Skegness Telegraph* this morning. Corporate headquarters, in Paris, sent me here to help with the rationalization." She rolled the word around her mouth, tongue darting out, licking her red lipstick.

The room fell quiet apart from the shuffling of nervous feet. My own shuffled so fast I was almost dancing, and it wasn't for joy.

"You," the witch said, pointing directly at yours truly. "Do you make a habit of arriving to work late?"

A drop of sweat slipped between my shoulder blades as my heart pounded, mind raced, and mouth said, "It's my second day, ma'am."

"A newbie, eh? Well, I expect my staff to be punctual." She jabbed her finger in the general direction of everyone. "Is that clear?"

"Yes, ma'am," we said in unison.

Lucy's lips tugged upward. The hairs on her chin jiggled. "Mr Paddington."

Ian shuffled forward. "Yes?"

"You have an announcement."

"Must I?"

The steely-grey eyes narrowed. "Do it!"

"Yes, ma'am," he said, his face a fearful mask of shock and defeat. "Fellow journalists, please raise your hand if you've worked at the newspaper over ten years."

Eagerly eight of the gathered crowd raised their hands. I wanted to raise mine too. I might have if I hadn't had to admit this was my second day. The other non-hand raisers looked like they shared my thoughts.

Mr Paddington straightened his back. "Every one of you old-timers knows how this paper works, understands the heartbeat of our easy-going community. Those of you with less experience..."

This is it, I thought, and knew what was coming next. I needed no dictionary to understand what rationalization meant—last in, first out. Rivulets of sweat trickled down my back. The rhythmic thud of blood pumping through my heart filled my ears. I gritted my teeth, wondered if there were any vacancies at Fantasy Gardens hot dog stand. It was closed until the tourist season, so I'd be without cash until the end of the month. Then I'd have to fight off the secondary school students for the job. There's no shame in flipping hot dogs when there are car mechanics and rent to pay.

"You have all given a great deal to the continuity of the newspaper..." Ian droned on. "The fabric of our community—"

Lucy stood up and slapped Ian on the back. "Enough platitudes. I'm afraid the rationalization begins today. I won't use the word 'fire,' but you old-timers can sling your hook." She turned to Ian. "And that includes you, Mr Paddington."

Chapter 5

A STUNNED SILENCE FILLED the room. No sound of feet shuffling—nothing. I'm cold and as still as a statue, waiting to see what happens next.

Lucy Baxter waved her hand in a dramatic flourish as if sending out a secret signal. Fred trotted forward, fleshy lips grinning, cardboard boxes in hand.

"You have ten minutes to clear your desks," he crowed handing out the boxes. One for each of the eight old-timers. "Miss Baxter instructed me to oversee your packing and dismissal from the building."

Without a word being exchanged, the old-timers shuffled out of the office with Fred out front like the lead hound pulling a dog sled.

Our eyes turned to Ian, who hadn't moved from the side of the desk. His large eyes bloodshot, head hung low like an over-ripe pear. He had aged ten years. Saddened and confused, I felt tears well up in my eyes and sniffed to hold back more.

"Firing me was a joke, right?" said Ian, turning to Lucy Baxter. "Funny sense of humour. Ha, ha, ha."

Lucy moved to sit down at his desk. Then stared at the man for several seconds and burst out laughing.

Encouraged, Ian's head tilted upward, his back straightened. "Ha, ha, hilarious. ha, ha." But there was an edge to his voice, a sense of desperation in his large brown eyes.

From his actions, I understood one thing—Ian needed the job as much as the rest of us. We were the survivors, the chosen few, destined to keep the *Skegness Telegraph* alive. The whole incident left a bittersweet taste in my mouth.

"Ha, ha, ha," Ian continued, stomach shaking, moving restlessly from leg to leg. "Miss Baxter, you almost got me there. Ha, ha."

With a quick nod of the head, Lucy indicated we join in. Like the rest of the survivors, I took part in the merry cackle even though I felt like throwing up. Every one of us had bills to pay. It felt like the first time Toby found me in a drunken stupor on the living room sofa. I'll never forget the look of disappointment in his eyes.

My drinking began in the empty days between freelance writing assignments. A single lunchtime glass of wine morphed into two, then three. Soon I was drinking a bottle or two with lunch and in the mornings—Beefeater Gin. I couldn't get through the day without a drink. Sleeping without a pill was impossible.

I was an alcoholic.

I was a drug addict.

Toby, anxious and vigilant, supported me the best a loving husband could. The more he tried to help, the harder I drank and the more pills I swallowed. I drove him away, filed for divorce, kept taking the pills and drinking.

Lucy's harsh laughter jolted me out of my thoughts. Three minutes had passed. Her arm continued to wave urging the laughter on. This isn't right, I thought, but continued with the artificial merrymaking.

With another flourish of her hand Lucy Baxter made an ugly snort. It sent a chill down my spine. She was smiling as she said, "Mr Paddington, the *Skegness Telegraph* is not making enough money."

"Profits are down for all print newspapers. Everything is going electronic," Ian replied. "Fortunately, the *Skegness Telegraph* has a loyal reader base. Circulation may not be improving year over year, but it's not shrinking either."

"Mr Paddington, I'm not here to discuss the decline in sales. Corporate headquarters sent me to turn this ship around. A newspaper of this size only needs a handful of staff."

Something must have snapped in Ian for he straightened his back and held his head erect. "The *Skegness Telegraph* has always provided news, entertainment, employment, and generated a reasonable profit. There is no doubt we can do it for the new owner. I urge you to reconsider letting go of eight of our seasoned employees."

Lucy Baxter gave Ian a searching look. "Porcherie Media Corporation does not acquire local newspapers to make a reasonable profit. It does not acquire newspapers to generate jobs. It acquires newspapers to make extraordinary profits."

"Of course," Ian replied, stumbling over his words, head dropping, back arching into a question mark. Like an outclassed boxer going the final round, he'd given up the fight. "If that is your final word on the matter."

"Indeed it is." Lucy jabbed her finger in the air, all the while a quiet smile kissed her lips. "There is only one way to maximize profits—squeeze down costs. I'm letting you go."

With another flourish of the hand, somewhat like a magician, she produced a cardboard box. On the side in a bold black pen were the letters *R.I.P.*

"This is for you," Lucy said with a chuckle. "Fred put your initials on the side. You've got thirty seconds to pack up, then Fred will see you out."

As we watched, wide-eyed, Ian scampered around the room like a stricken rabbit picking up items and tossing them into the box.

"Time's up!" Lucy roared as Fred reappeared, his fleshy lips curved into a catlike smirk.

"Fred, please escort Mr Rupert Ian Paddington from our premises."

"Yes, ma'am. This way, Mr Paddington."

Chapter 6

IAN'S FACE WAS A PICTURE of abject misery as he shuffled out of his office. Thirty-five years of memories stuffed into a tiny cardboard box. There and then I wanted to quit. But reality sealed my mouth—the rent was due, the car needed fixing, and I had to eat. There was no choice. I'd have to tough it out at the *Skegness Telegraph* until I'd saved enough money to break free. As I glanced around at the surviving journalists, I saw similar ideas bubbling behind their shocked eyes.

The rest of the day was a haze. Head office called in via Skype for a motivational team meeting.

"Lucy Baxter is creating zee future for zee *Skegness Telegraph*," the chief executive officer boomed. He spoke with a heavy French accent and at times was difficult to understand. "As you know she is an, une fille locale; how you say in English—a local girl. If vous want to be part of notre succès let me vous jump up and twirl around."

We were on our feet, spinning around like whirling dervishes.

"Très bon, zat is good. I can zee Lucy has already crafted a motivated team."

Then we set to work producing the newspaper. The funny thing is, it came out on time looking like any other edition of the *Skegness Telegraph*.

"The secret to my amazing success," Lucy said, as we gathered around her in the newsroom, "is my incredible dedication to the newspaper industry. I put in the hours and have reaped the rewards. I like to arrive about twelve thirty a.m. and work till around four in the morning. Then it's home for a short nap and back at my desk by eight thirty. Any questions?"

There was a general reluctance to raise one's hand in Lucy's presence on account it might be bitten off. That didn't stop me. "What do you do in your spare time?"

"Teach kung fu."

The room went silent, partly in sheer awe of Wonder Woman, and in fear that she'd expect us to work her hours and take up the martial arts. I needed the job, would do what I could to keep it, and made a mental note to look up karate classes at the community centre.

"Any other questions?"

Nothing.

"Good. Everyone must leave the office before I finish for the day," Lucy told us. "Seven is when I'm done tonight. Please leave the building by six fifty-five. Do I make myself clear?"

It was around half past six when Lucy fired Fred, replacing him with a contracted security firm. She insisted we gather in the lobby as he was marched from the premises. Unlike Fred, who remained at his desk reading the newspaper and drinking tea, the new guy patrolled the building.

"I'm digging up the weeds and tossing them out," Lucy said when Fred was gone. "If you don't like my methods, please leave now. Any takers?"

No one responded. Nothing but the sound of shuffling feet.

At six fifty-five everyone left the building like bullets out of a gun. No doubt to race home and begin their Google search for another job. The sun had set, street lights were already on, and a light breeze held back the rain. It wasn't until I was in the car park, at my usual space, that I remembered the Micra was still in the driveway of Whispering Towers Boarding House. Now it was too late to wave down one of my co-workers.

I pulled out my mobile phone to call Harry Sutton Town-Wide Minicabs. A flicker of movement caught my eyes. From the shadow at the side of the building, a figure emerged.

I prepared to run.

"Doris, is that you?" The figure moved forward. Under the glow of the street lamp, I realized it was Ian.

"What are you doing here?" A lame question, but all I could manage at the end of an exhausting day.

Ian was at my side now. The sour odour of alcohol filled the evening air. "My Joyce. I forgot my Joyce." He said the words in a sorrowful wail. "Married thirty-nine years. Met her at elementary school, best friends, lovers, later husband and wife—no kids."

I placed an arm around his shoulder. "Ian, it's been a challenging day. Time to go home. Joyce will wonder where you are."

His large brown eyes filled with tears which ran down his cheeks and dribbled down his chin. "Joyce won't be at home. She died last month, cancer."

It was a moment where the only thing to say is nothing. Reaching out I gave Ian a hug. Together, we stood in silence clinging on to fading memories of lost loved ones.

Eventually we separated. "Doris," he said, swaying from side to side, "I left the photo of my Joyce on the office desk."

"I remember the photo. Swirly gold leaves and a dark-haired woman in a blue summer smock?"

"That's my Joyce. The witch can't have it! I'm getting it back, now."

That didn't sound like a good idea. How would Ian get by the security guard? They'd catch him. Lucy Baxter would delight in pressing charges. A rush of anger surged through me like an electric current: anger at Ian for not having the courage to stand up to Lucy Baxter, at the *Skegness Telegraph* which had trapped me like a caged Bengal tiger, and at myself for not telling Lucy Baxter where she could shove the job in the first place.

I made an instant decision. "Wait here. The photograph is still in your old office. I'll sneak in and get it."

He nodded, tears filling his eyes.

"God bless you, Doris."

Chapter 7

QUICKLY I MOVED TOWARDS the building, peered through the glass doors into the reception area. It was empty. "The security guard must be on his rounds."

I pressed the door handle followed by a gentle push, and I was in the lobby area. My heart raced as I hurried inside. Half expecting an alarm to sound, I kept close to the wall, but I could do nothing about the bright lights illuminating the place.

The newsroom was beyond another glass door. From there I'd have easy access to Ian's old office. I leaned against the door, peering into the newsroom. It was dark with no signs of movement. Maybe the security guard was outside? That thought gave me a jolt. If he came back now, I'd be a sitting duck.

I pulled at the door handle, then pushed.

It was locked.

For an instant I was ready to give up, get out of the place before I was spotted. Then I remembered the buzzer. Fred had pressed it to let me into the newsroom. I circled around the security desk. There it was.

I pressed.

There was a slight sound as the door to the newsroom clicked open.

I hurried to the door and pushed.

It swung gently open.

With caution, I stepped into the darkened room. A dusty smell mixed with a faint odour of coffee filled my nose. The low lights cast creepy shadows in every direction. Where was the security guard?

To keep out of sight, I crouched low in the first cubical, listening for every creak, every sound. There was nothing. No voices, no footsteps, not even the squeak of a door.

Keeping low and close to the wall I made my way to Ian's old office.

The door was shut.

Locked?

I reached out, pressed the handle. The rusty squeak roared out like an alarm bell.

I froze, again listening—nothing.

Still gazing around I leaned into the door, pushing gently. It opened fully without another sound.

A single lamp illuminated the room, enough to see by. Remaining crouched, I looked over at the desk where Ian had kept the photograph of Joyce. It was gone. I padded across the room, stood behind the desk, and again scanned the room. Where is it?

Doubt tumbled into my mind. Ian's breath oozed with alcohol. Suppose drink had given him the idea Joyce's photograph was missing when it was really in his box?

"Oh bugger!"

For several moments I tossed the idea around in my mind. It had been three months since I'd had a drink, but even when drunk, I knew the difference between reality and fantasy. Ian's concern was genuine. I sensed it.

"The photograph is in here somewhere."

Carefully, I eased down into the executive chair. The desk surface was clear of papers. Only a lamp and a heavy paperweight. On the left side was a drawer. I tugged. It slipped open with ease. On top, a handwritten note on headed paper—*Fiddles and Tweedles* in bold black letters. For a moment I read the scrawling script, then gave up. The framed photograph was underneath. Disturbing nothing else, I grabbed it and darted out of the room.

I would make it.

As I hurried across the newsroom, I heard footsteps clattering on the concrete floor like pistol cracks.

It was the security guard.

I darted into the nearest cubical, crouched low, heart pumping like crazy, sour sensation in the pit of my stomach. What would I say if the security guard spotted me?

The footsteps grew louder. They were coming in my direction. I crouched lower.

Clack, clack, clack.

I could hear them more clearly. I flattened myself on the floor, peering through the crack at the bottom of the cubical wall.

A flashlight flicked on.

Shiny black boots stopped at the cubical.

My lungs felt like they would explode, but I dared not breathe. If the security guard caught me, Lucy Baxter would fire me. Visions of working the Fantasy Gardens hot dog stand filled my mind.

But there was a chance I'd make it out of here.

"You can come out now."

Caught. I couldn't move, waiting for the hand on my shoulder. I'd failed in this as I had in my marriage. It was I who turned to drink; I who took the pills; I who asked for the divorce. I should have called the cab and gone home, told Ian to do the same. He'd sober up in the morning, probably not even remember his photograph was missing.

The voice spoke again, louder. "I said you can come out now."

I opened my eyes.

The boots moved away.

"Yes... you can come out now... How long will you be?... Thirty minutes... Okay... It's all quiet here... Yes, okay... I'm checking out now, then... I'll leave the lights on in the lobby... The regular shift change after tonight will be at midnight... Bye."

A door slammed.

After five minutes I sat up, leaned against the side of the cubical, panting. Sweat trickled down my forehead, stinging my eyes. Then I got to my feet and hurried out of the building.

LATER THAT NIGHT I stood by my bedsit window, beer can in hand and looked down into the street. I remembered my promise to call Toby. There was so much to be curious about, so much I wanted to know. Who is Norah Porlock? Why is Leo Warrington pestering her, and is he really associated with criminal gangs and violent? Tonight, those questions would remain unanswered. Even though Toby was waiting, I wouldn't call.

A cat slinked along the gutter on the hunt for prey. I wondered what it felt like to be an animal trapped by instinct and at the beck and call of Mother Nature.

Always searching for food.

Always on the lookout for predators.

Always on the run.

I opened the beer can.

The hoppy smell floated up like the sweet aroma of French perfume. Pressed to my lips, I knew it would lift the heavy feeling weighing down my heart. Knew I wouldn't stop at one; knew in the morning I'd wake full of regret from my broken promises.

"To change your life, you have to change your habits," the leader of the Alcoholics Anonymous group had said.

"But how do you change your habits?" I had asked.

"One day at a time."

I turned from the window and walked to the kitchen.

"I want to change," I said, emptying the can into the sink. "I want to get better."

Chapter 8

THE WEDDING WAS AT noon that Saturday, a bright blustery day with a clear blue sky and little chance of rain. As Mrs Lintott and I hurried through the car park towards the entrance of the Hidden Caves Chapel, she said, "Doris, you didn't answer my question."

With a puzzled expression, I replied, "What question?"

"About Toby Cudlow. Is he your brother or a relative?"

I kept walking as I answered, looking straight ahead. "Neither, Toby's my ex-husband. For the record, we divorced after ten years—no kids."

Mrs Lintott shook her head. "He must've been a fool to throw aside a woman like you."

We hurried by an ambulance with two uniformed men standing stiffly by the back doors, eyes on the chapel entrance, then up a handful of steps to the doorway of the chapel. It was once part of a monastery and set into a cliff overlooking a sandy beach one hundred and fifty feet below. The only entrance was through an arched doorway shielded by a heavy wooden, medieval-style door. The chapel seated around seventy-five people.

Guests were settling into their seats as Mrs Lintott and I stood at the entrance peering inside. There were no windows.

Light came from electric lanterns attached at regular spaces along the walls. They flickered like Roman candles casting a gloomy glow. Even from the open doorway, the place smelled like an antique furniture store.

"It's a sight to behold, like one of those wonders of the world," said Mrs Lintott in awe. Then after a moment or two she added, "You know, it's a little too much like Batman's lair for my taste. I hope the rector has his reading glasses."

A plume of tobacco drifted in our direction. Coughing, I spun around to identify the source. A slender man stood ten feet away under the branches of a tall tree, smoking. He wore a dark navy-blue, pinstriped suit, black-and-white shoes, and a grey fedora tipped back exposing cold, blue eyes. With each new puff of smoke, he glanced anxiously out at the ambulance and then to the entrance of the chapel.

"Leo Warrington," Mrs Lintott whispered, eyeing the man with caution. "He's plumb bad, like one of those maggot-ridden apples that makes the others rotten."

So, this was the infamous Leo Warrington. Toby had described him as a gangster, and he looked the part. All that was missing was a machine gun.

Leo dropped the cigarette butt and stomped it with his foot. In an almost continuous movement he rolled another and lit it. Despite the decidedly cool breeze, a sheen of perspiration glistened on his forehead which he wiped with a handkerchief, his hands moving in little jerks and twitches.

A pang of guilt washed over me. I hadn't even attempted to investigate Leo's background although I promised Toby I'd do a little digging. I knew he did some sort of manual work, but that was about it. The daily hell of working for Lucy Baxter at the *Skegness Telegraph* sucked all my energy. It had only been two days, but it felt like eternity. My early attempts at finding another job had turned up nothing. Now, though, I wanted to find out more about Leo and expected, with a little prodding, Mrs Lintott would tell all she knew.

"What have you got on Leo?"

Mrs Lintott's nose wrinkled. "I don't like to speak ill of people, so I'll say no more."

That was a new one on me. She always gossiped. I tried a different angle. "What is his relationship to Norah?"

She sucked in a sharp breath. "He who plays with fire dies by fire," she answered with a mysterious twinkle in her eyes. "Come on, Doris. Let's get inside." And without another word, she slipped into the arched entrance.

We stood at the back of the chapel amidst a cluster of peach-clad bridesmaids. It took a moment for my eyes to adjust to the gloom and another moment to realize, except for two small girls, the bridesmaids appeared to be in their seventies.

As if reading my mind Mrs Lintott said, "The rector's girls, from the Golden Shores Elderly Home. He brings them along when he officiates a wedding. It gives the retired ladies something to do, and they help keep things flowing smoothly. The maid of honour and flower girls are all family of the bridesmaids. Oh, look, there's the rector." She pointed to a big, heavy-set man wearing black robes at the front of the church. My heart skipped a beat—he was talking to Toby.

Even from the back of the church, and through the gloom, I could see Toby was smiling. He looked relaxed and happy, just as I remembered him. An almost overwhelming urge overcame me—run to the front of the church, grab him by the shoulders and tell him. Tell him what?

"Excuse me, ladies," a man said, shoving by. "I'm going to bring an end to this wedding fiasco."

His back arched, and he carried a cane in his right hand. I could tell by the thin, wayward strands of jet-white hair sticking out of his tartan flat cap he wasn't in the first bloom of youth; he wasn't in the second bloom either.

"Oh no," one of the elderly bridesmaids yelled, "That's him. That's Reggie Porlock."

The man was making his way to the front of the chapel. It wasn't a march or even a fast walk, more like a determined shuffle.

"Reggie," one of the bridesmaid's called. "Come back here!"

He halted, slowly turned around and waved his walking stick in the air. His old stone-grey eyes flashed with bitterness. "The wedding can't happen today. Norah Porlock is married. She's my wife."

Chapter 9

A SEA OF PEACH BRIDESMAIDS hurried after Reggie. A look of mischievous disbelief filled his face as they surrounded him. Then, like sheepdogs rounding up a stray lamb, they hustled him towards the entrance and out of the chapel.

"Oooh, Doris, now they're letting the loonies loose!" cried Mrs Lintott, clapping her hands. "This is better than watching a soap opera on the telly." She held her mobile phone high in the air. "Got some good photos of the bridesmaids chasing the old bloke out. Wait till I tell the ladies at the bingo club; they'll be green with envy, and we haven't even got to the main ceremony yet."

Part of me wanted the stooped old man to have made it to the altar. Then the wedding might have been called off or delayed. Another part of me felt terrible for wishing ill of Norah's big day. "Do you think there is any truth in what Reggie said?"

Mrs Lintott touched my arm. "Doris, it can be quite traumatic, weddings. Lots of tears." Her voice softened. "It can't be easy watching your husband remarry. You still love him, don't you?"

I closed my eyes, drawing deep from reserves, of which I had been unaware, to steady my nerves. Once the butterflies had settled, I said, "We got married straight out of college. Things didn't work out."

"Will you be all right? We can go now, if you want."

"No. I'm fine." I wasn't, but said, "My marriage to Toby is history. His future belongs to Norah Porlock."

"Really? Old flames burn the brightest, they say." Mrs Lintott frowned. "Ten years together is a long time. You gave him everything, and now he gets the girl, and you're living in my bedsit. That's not right!"

I changed the subject for fear of breaking out into wild sobs. "So, who do you think the old man, Reggie, is?"

"Probably her granddad. Yes, that must be it, and he is upset over losing his granddaughter to your ex-hubby. I've seen it before. Very emotional; a good wedding touches my heart every time."

An usher started down the aisle with Toby's parents. My heart was beating like a drum as they strode by. I shrunk back, fearful they would recognize me. But they looked straight ahead walking at a steady pace towards the front.

"Here Comes the Bride" drifted through hidden speakers. Remembering my wedding day, I began to cry and turned to look at the back of the church. There she was: Norah Porlock, in a gorgeous white dress with a long flowing train, the veil drawn down over her face.

The ushers were at the altar, followed by the bridesmaids, and four tiny flower girls. The maid of honour followed, and then as I glanced around for another look at the bride, there was the wail of an ambulance followed by a loud creak as a door to the chapel swung shut. Then the lights went out.

It was several moments before a growing murmur filled the chapel, and Rector Beasley called out for calm. "A temporary electricity blackout. There is no need for alarm. Please remain in your seats, and they will restore the lights in short order."

It was unnerving sitting in the pitch black listening to the low mumble of anxious voices. I could sense Mrs Lintott next to me but saw little else.

"Open the doors. Can someone open the doors, please," boomed the rector. "We need light in here."

From the back of the church came the cry, "We've already tried, but someone jammed the lock."

The mumble of voices grew louder, more anxious. "Everything's gonna be all right," I could hear Toby saying. "It's just a minor hiccup in the road."

But the voices grew louder, more distinct.

"Let me out of here," someone cried into the blackness.

"Me too," added another.

Gradually, like stars appearing in a night-time sky, mobile phone screens flickered on. Collectively, they generated enough light to see.

At the front, Toby stood next to the rector and the best man. He was saying something, arms moving about wildly, head twisting as if looking in all directions. I wanted to get up and give him a hug, let him know everything would be all right.

Toby pointed towards the back of the chapel. I swivelled around to look. There didn't appear to be anything out of the ordinary. Then I glanced along the aisle scanning the pews all the way to the altar. The maid of honour, peach bridesmaids, and flower girls were together in one group. But something was missing.

Mrs Lintott grabbed my arm, her voice sharp with alarm. "Doris, what's happened to the bride? Where is Norah Porlock?"

Chapter 10

THERE WAS NO SIGN OF Norah in the church and when over an hour later help arrived to open the heavy wooden door, there was no sign of her in the car park either. Under the branches of a tall tree, the rector wrapped an arm around Toby's shoulder and spoke to him earnestly. A few steps away, the best man shuffled nervously.

"It's like an episode of *Dr. Who*," Mrs Lintott said, reaching into her handbag and pulling out a pink hip flask. She took a long slow sip. "Scotland's finest. Go on, Doris. Take a swig. You need it."

I placed the flask to my lips, then I remembered. "No, thank you, Mrs Lintott." I didn't want to offend, so I made an excuse. "With the electricity cutting out, doors mysteriously locked, and the bride vanishing in thin air, I need to keep my wits about me."

Mrs Lintott chuckled, took another swig. "The ladies at the bingo club will never believe this. I may as well get tipsy."

Another hour passed before most of the guests drifted away, and almost an hour after that a police officer arrived. His name was Constable Wriggly, a plump man in his early forties who I later learned had a reputation for saying, "I'm off-duty, Sergeant," or "It's not up to me; ask the person in charge."

A small crowd of bridesmaids and relatives remained around Toby, including the rector and the best man. I hung out near the back, out of Toby's sight, curious to hear what the police officer would say.

"The Lincolnshire Constabulary is on your side, but I don't understand," Constable Wriggly said when Toby had finished. "Vanished in thin air?"

"Yes. Norah disappeared as the ceremony was about to begin. The lights went out, the chapel door slammed shut, and then...she vanished."

"Ah ha!" Constable Wriggly said, ignoring Toby's last sentence, "You mean you saw Norah leave?"

"No, she *vanished*."

The constable looked perplexed, eyed Toby with concern. "If you like, you can file a missing person's report. Better to wait forty-eight hours, though. Now, if you don't mind, I'll head back to the station, it's almost time for the shift change."

"Listen. Someone has kidnapped Norah," wailed Toby. "Constable Wriggly, what are you going to do about it?"

"Now, sir, let's not jump to conclusions. You're in a very emotional state and jumping to conclusions won't help matters. I suggest you go home, get a nice cuppa and a sausage roll, and visit the police station in the morning to file a missing person's report."

"Aren't you going to look for my Norah now?" Toby's eyes were wide with anguish.

Constable Wriggly shook his head. "That won't be necessary, sir."

"Why not?"

"It's not up to me. I'll have to ask my superior officer."

"What? You have discretion, man. Use it!"

The constable cleared his throat. "Yes, sir, I am. I don't like to be the harbinger of bad news, sir, but it is clear what happened here."

The crowd leaned forward, eager to hear the constable's interpretation.

"An old story," the constable continued, shaking his head, enjoying the attention. "I reckon we get two or three every year in town; hard to believe, but that's the facts." He halted, glanced around at the eager eyes, then smiled as if he held some great secret.

"Please continue," Toby said, eyes filled with hope. "You've seen it before? What have you seen? Will it help us find Norah?"

"Sir, what I have to tell you will hurt." The constable placed a hand to his cheek as if considering how he should proceed. "It won't do you no good to keep the truth hidden, I suppose. Here is what happened. I won't mention any names to soften the blow a little. The bride gets cold feet, see? And she bolts, leaving the groom stranded at the altar. Sad to say it happens the other way around too. I'm sorry for you, sir."

"No!" cried Toby. "Something terrible has happened. I insist you investigate, now."

The constable gave a sigh of exasperation. "Sir, the Lincolnshire Constabulary is on your side. But our hands are tied until you file a missing person's report...in say, forty-eight hours. Now, I suggest you go home, grab a cuppa, and sausage roll. I must be on my way."

The rector placed an arm around Toby's shoulder, then turned to the police officer. "Constable Wriggly, I have officiated numerous weddings at this venue. You are aware of that, aren't you?"

The constable nodded. "Of that I am, Rector."

The Rector removed his arm from Toby's shoulder. "I officiated the wedding of Inspector Doxon. You remember that, don't you?"

The constable shifted his feet. "Yes, a wonderful wedding."

"Inspector Doxon is a good friend."

"Indeed, sir."

"Let me tell you what I saw, given you haven't asked."

Constable Wriggly let out a quiet sigh. "Please do."

The rector took in a long deep breath, scanned the faces of the gathered crowd, and seemed suddenly energized.

"I was discussing the finer points of the wedding ceremony with Mr Cudlow and the best man when the music began. As you know the music signifies the bride's arrival." He was talking fast now as if giving a fiery sermon from the pulpit. "As I glanced towards the back of the chapel, I saw a bloom of peach bridesmaids, a ripple of flower girls, the maid of honour...and behold the bride in all her glory. The music continued softly as the future wife of Mr Cudlow floated down the aisle. Not that I could see her face, but I know it was angelic. Then, as if the stars had fallen from the sky, the chapel turned black. An instant later the dim light of mobile phones broke through the darkness." His voice rose to a dramatic crescendo. "But the bride was gone!"

"I see, sir," Constable Wriggly said, rubbing his chin.

The rector slammed his right fist into the palm of his left. "Isn't that exactly what Toby Cudlow has already said?"

"Quite so, but your version has a rather dramatic flourish."

"Constable Wriggly, everyone saw what I described." The rector spun around jabbing his finger at the gathered crowd. "Anyone see anything different?"

There was a loud murmur of agreement followed by applause.

The rector turned back to the constable, eyes glaring like globes of fire. "Constable, what are you going to do?"

Constable Wriggly ran a hand through his hair, but all he managed was, "I see, I see."

"I'll ask the question again," the rector said in a booming voice. "What are you going to do about it?"

"I'll take a statement," Constable Wriggly said hesitatingly. "Then I'll file a report."

"No!" boomed the rector.

"No?" asked Constable Wriggly.

"You will find out the source of the electricity failure, find out who bolted the chapel door shut, but first, you will search the chapel for clues. The investigation into the disappearance of Norah Porlock begins here, and now!"

The constable fell silent for a moment. Then, as if the idea was his own said, "Please stay out of the chapel. I will search for clues." His eyes narrowed. "Nobody leaves until I'm done."

Chapter 11

WHEN CONSTABLE WRIGGLY, the rector, and Toby had disappeared inside the chapel, Mrs Lintott said, "Doris, I'll wait in the car. Join me when you're ready."

That was my cue to leave, to get away from the crowd, but I didn't go with my gut; instead, I lingered—big mistake.

"Doris, is that you?" The voice came from behind. I knew who it was before I turned to look. Mrs Margaret Cudlow, Toby's mum.

"Doris, what a pleasure to see you. How are you doing?" The smile did not extend to her eyes.

"Hello, Margaret," I said in a cheery voice. "Nice day, isn't it?"

"Travel from London?" she asked in a frosty tone.

"I live in Skegness, work for the local paper."

"That must be nice for you. Pleased to hear you are doing something...positive."

I tried my best *let bygones be bygones* voice. "Are you and Mr Cudlow keeping well?"

"The weather is nice; isn't it, dear?"

I gave up. "Yes, lovely for this time of year."

Margaret sniffed. "Are you still writing? How's the novel coming along? Finished yet?"

"Not much progress to report there. Too busy."

"Exciting social life, I expect. Out all hours, eh?"

"Not really, still settling into seaside life. Skegness is a nice little town."

Again she sniffed. "That must be lovely for you, dear."

"Things are not easy, but I'm getting on my feet."

"Getting on your feet! Doris, I wish I could say the same for Toby," she said, her voice low so as not to be overheard. "Well, you've got a nerve showing up here today, after all you put my son through, after everything he did for you."

I gulped hard, swallowing back a tear. "Life's not been easy for me, you know."

"They say it's the easiest thing in the world, to turn to drink when the going gets tough. Pop another pill rather than face reality. Why did you do it? Why did you break my son's heart and destroy his life?"

I didn't answer. How could I explain? The drinking wasn't about Toby, it was about me. Same with the pills. And his life was far from destroyed. He'd met a new bride, lived in a ritzy neighbourhood in London while I struggled in Skegness.

"If you'd stayed off the drink, you'd be happily married to a doting husband," Mrs Cudlow continued. "Toby would be his old self, and I'd have a grandchild or two instead of—"

"Doris! Toby told me you might attend," said Mr Malcolm Cudlow, Toby's dad. He glanced at his wife's face, then at me. "You have a special place in our hearts. I hope you have faced down your demons. Let's let bygones be bygones."

Malcolm Cudlow always had a unique way with words. Even when he discovered I was drinking and on drugs, he always encouraged, never criticized, never condemned, and never complained. I wished for the thousandth time I had chosen a different path, but I'd made my bed and was lying in it.

"If it wasn't for her drinking, we'd have grandchildren," sobbed Mrs Cudlow. "You know how much that means. Now, it's too late."

"Come on, Margaret, let's wait for news in our car," Malcolm said, taking his wife by the arm and leading her away. When they were ten feet away, he turned and said, "Take care of yourself, Doris. Our address and telephone number haven't changed. Please write or call."

Most of the remaining guests had wandered back to their cars. I needed to be alone, couldn't face any questioning from Mrs Lintott, wanted to remain under the bright clear sky with that cool breeze chasing away my thoughts. I watched the waves crashing gently on the shore. A flock of seagulls scoured the beach for food, and a lone figure walked a black and white dog.

"Doris!"

Toby rushed forward, sweeping me into his arms. There was no time to react, no time to compose my thoughts. My legs felt like jelly, and butterflies danced in my stomach as I returned his hug. "I'm sorry about Norah," I said, and I meant it.

"Today has been terrible," he sobbed quietly into my ear. "Wish it was over, but seeing you has—"

"Absolutely nothing," interrupted the rector, joining us. Alongside him was Constable Wriggly. We broke off and turned to hear what they had to say.

"How is it there are no clues?" the rector demanded, turning to the constable. "And you a fully trained officer of the Lincolnshire Constabulary?"

Constable Wriggly rubbed the back of his neck. "If there had been an abduction, I'm sure I would have spotted something. The constabulary runs a course on crime scene investigation. I'm a graduate, and I got to say, there is little out of the ordinary in this case." He sounded confident now, his hands on his hips. "There has been no crime committed; no cause for alarm. Rector, this whole incident is little more than a runaway bride."

"What about the power outage?" the rector asked, his voice not as strident as before.

"An act of fate, hand of God, if you will."

The rector hesitated a moment, then said, "What about the bolted door? Someone tampered with the lock."

"A simple prank, played by a friend of the groom, I expect," Constable Wriggly replied in an authoritative tone. "Surely, Rector, a man of your experience has seen such pranks before."

"Sure have," the rector mumbled, rubbing his temples. "But this takes the biscuit."

Constable Wriggly turned to Toby. "Mr Cudlow, why don't you give it a day or so? Norah will be in touch, I'm sure. Now, are you ready for a cuppa and a sausage roll?"

Rector Beasley placed an arm around Toby's shoulder. "Son, it's time to go home."

"No!" Toby said, his eyes darting around wildly from the rector to the constable. He wasn't crying, but he wasn't far from it. "Today was her big day. Why would she run?"

Constable Wriggly softened his voice. "Norah changed her mind, sir. This is a free country. She'll show up in the morning."

Chapter 12

IT WAS THE FOLLOWING morning when the call came through. I was in my cubicle at the *Skegness Telegraph* on a tight deadline for an article about the opening of Fantasy Gardens for the new season, and I still had to track down the owner, Mr Doug Hornsby, for an interview. Then there was the afternoon one-to-one meeting with Lucy Baxter at 3 p.m. I still hadn't prepared for that either.

"Hello," I said, picking up my mobile phone without checking the screen. A bad habit I'm trying to correct.

"Doris, it's Toby." From the tone of his voice, the news wasn't good.

"What is it?" I said with a sense of unease, almost foreboding.

"They found Norah."

"Where? Is she all right?"

"I can't talk here. I'm in town. Can you meet me in thirty minutes at the Fiddlers Bowl for an early lunch?"

This lunchtime I'd planned on eating at my desk, using the extra seconds between bites to prepare for my meeting with Lucy Baxter. Since the mechanic patched up my Micra, I had wheels as well as another bill. A quick lunch with Toby, and I'd be back at my desk in time to scribble down a few notes ahead of my meeting with the new boss. "I'll be at a table by the window."

Fiddlers Bowl was a busy and dim, small café tucked into a side alley off Prince George Street. The usual mix of locals and workmen hunched over plastic tables with red-white-and-blue faded tablecloths. The air was thick with a dozen simultaneous conversations, although none complaining about the food which was homemade and good.

I found Toby at a window table staring at the menu. His ashen face and sunken eyes told me all I needed to know. Without a word, I slipped into a seat opposite and said a silent prayer hoping he would not say what I feared. He began to speak before I'd said hello.

"Norah's body washed up on the beach about a mile away from the Hidden Caves Chapel." He looked down at his hands as he spoke. "Just back from the morgue...a ghastly experience... Norah's face... There wasn't much of it left."

"Ready to order?" said a cheerful teenager with silver braces. "The special today is chicken pot pie with steamed vegetables and chips or mash."

Toby nodded mutely, took on his old role and ordered for us both. "Yes, we'll go for that—mashed potatoes."

"So, that's the special with mash, twice?" She smiled.

He let out a heavy breath. "Yes."

The teenager scurried to the kitchen.

Now, I was quaking inside, barely able to form thoughts let alone words. "Toby, what happened?" I stuttered at last.

Before he answered, the sound of loud voices came from the counter.

"All I want is a job. I'll take anything," wailed a male voice. I recognized the voice and the man behind it. Fred, the security guard from the *Skegness Telegraph*.

"Get out of here. I got all the workers I need," yelled a thick-set man who looked like a cook.

Fred, shoulders slumped, turned and shuffled out of the café. "I ought to put a brick through your window," he muttered as he left. "Lived here all my life and all of those out-of-towners are taking the jobs!"

As the café door swung shut, people returned to their conversations and Toby continued. "A local walking their dog found Norah's remains yesterday evening. The police called, and I came down by train this morning. Visited the morgue for identification." Toby's hands moved restlessly, toying with a fork, then clawing at his face before rubbing his eyes with balled fists. "Norah was still wearing her wedding dress."

In the partial light of the café Toby's face had a ghostly pallor, and the corners of his mouth turned down like an inverted horseshoe. He looked as miserable as the day I asked for the divorce.

"Here you go," the waitress said. "Two specials, lots of mash. Can I get you anything else?" The teenager glanced momentarily at our faces, then, without waiting for a response, hurried off to serve another table.

Toby licked his dry lips and leaned forward. "Inspector Doxon was with me when I identified the body..." His voice broke off in silent sobs.

I reached across the table to take his trembling hands in my own. They were warm and clammy. There was a hint of alcohol on his breath. "What is it Toby? What did the inspector say?"

His breath quickened, and his face flushed. "Norah was murdered. I'm not to leave town."

Tears blurred my eyes. "Surely they can't think you—"

"Toby Cudlow?" The question came from a baldheaded man in a crumpled brown suit, cream shirt, and plum-red tie. He looked like a worn-out comprehensive-school history teacher. Two uniformed officers stood at his side. I recognized one as Constable Wriggly.

"Inspector Doxon!" The surprise in Toby's voice was tinged with something else—resignation.

"Mr Cudlow, I'd like you to accompany me to the station."

"Why?" I asked on Toby's behalf.

"And you are?"

"Doris Cudlow," I said with a hiss. "And, yes, before you ask, I'm Toby's ex-wife."

The inspector's eyes narrowed. "I see. Live here in town, do you?"

"Yes, the Whispering Towers Boarding House. I'm a reporter at the *Skegness Telegraph*."

"Really. So you live in town, then?"

"What's it got to do with you?"

He smiled, turned to Toby. "Mr Cudlow, are you ready?"

"Am I under arrest?" Toby asked, voice trembling.

"If you don't come quietly, that will be the case."

The two uniformed officers stepped closer.

In that instant, it felt as if we were on the centre stage of a West End show. The cook and several of his helpers scurried out of the kitchen to gawp. An old man in a flat cloth cap and holding an unlit pipe shouted, "Another drug bust! And they look like a regular couple. Can't fool our coppers that easy!" But otherwise the room fell silent. All I could hear was a pounding of blood through my temples. And everyone's eyes watched, waiting to see what would happen next.

Toby stood up.

"Inspector Doxon, I'm ready," he said, giving a weak smile. "Ask me what you like; I've nothing to hide."

Chapter 13

"DORIS, I'M MEETING with every member of the team, and then I'll decide who to promote." Lucy Baxter had been speaking for ten minutes, but I hadn't heard a word. I was sitting in a hard-plastic chair in her office. "Do you have any questions?"

"No," I said meekly. "Very comprehensive, yes...very clear. No further questions required."

"I expect my employees to have questions in our one-to-one meetings," she said impatiently. "I know it's a change from the sloppy way Mr Paddington ran things, so I'll give you a moment." She drummed her fingers on her desk.

"Can you clarify your expectations?" I said, playing for time.

Lucy's brow creased. "Doris, that is what I have been doing for the past ten minutes. Have you been paying attention?" She didn't wait for an answer. "From now on, every reporter at the *Skegness Telegraph* must have one or two side stories—long-term projects they are working on. These stories will appear in the newspaper, and if they merit it, in Porcherie Media Corporation's other newspapers. Now, tell me about your side projects."

My special project involved searching for another job. "Well...I... I... err..."

Lucy Baxter flashed an icy stare. "Please go on. I'm all ears."

"The death of a bride-to-be," I stuttered, mind racing fast. "That's what I'm working on."

Lucy leaned forward. "Really? A recent death or from the archives?"

"So recent the police haven't announced it yet. The victim was a woman by the name of Norah Porlock. She disappeared during her wedding ceremony at the Hidden Caves Chapel."

"Interesting. Please go on."

"A local found the body yesterday evening."

"Where?"

"On a beach, a short distance away from the Hidden Caves Chapel."

"Suicide?"

"No, it was murder."

Lucy's eyebrows shot up. "Confirmed by the police?"

"Not yet."

"Any suspects?"

"They've taken her husband-to-be into custody." I didn't mention my relationship with Toby.

Lucy was silent for a long moment. "No offense to you or Norah, but all you've got is local interest, two lines tops in the police blotter section. It is the sort of story Mr Paddington would have published. That's why I had to get rid of him. The new *Skegness Telegraph* is more than a police blotter. Listen, I'm looking for stories with sizzle, stories that will grow our readership. Drop this one. What else have you got?"

That stunned me. My cheeks burned as if she'd slapped my face. And it hurt just as much. "A bride disappears from her wedding ceremony and washes up dead on the beach. How much more sizzle do you want?" My tone was belligerent, but I didn't care.

Lucy regarded me for a moment then blinked. "Doris, I'm not sure this is it, but here is what I want you to do." She raised a finger to her lips. "Keep working the bride story on the side. In the meantime, I'd like you to work on another side project. Mr Doug Hornsby claims his new fish-and-chip-flavoured hot dogs will be a runaway success. Give me a full report in, say, two weeks about the hot dogs, might even make the front page." There was a brisk note in her tone; the meeting was over.

As I walked to the door Lucy added, "Doris, I like you and have you marked down for a top spot. From now on, though, please stop by my office daily. I'd like updates on both your side projects."

Chapter 14

BACK IN MY CUBICAL, I called Toby's mobile phone. He didn't pick up. I left a message. Then opened a new notebook and made a few notes. What did I know about Norah Porlock? That she was Toby's wife-to-be. The thought made me feel grubby as if I was physically digging through another person's rubbish. An internet search revealed Norah worked as an auditor, but little else. She had no Facebook page or any other social media presence. I assumed they had met in London, but even that was a guess.

I tapped my pen on the notebook. "What else?"

I drew a blank and thought about the wedding. The bride in white, the flower girls, the bridesmaids and then the old man with the walking stick. Mrs Lintott thought he was a loony. I'd hardly given him a second thought. What was his name?

"Reggie...Reggie Porlock. Yes, that was it." He claimed to be Nora's husband, but that couldn't be right; he was simply too old. I drummed my fingers on the notebook. Suppose he was telling the truth, and they were man and wife? "No," I said again, "that makes little sense, best stick to the facts." On the first line of the notebook I wrote *Reggie Porlock—granddad?*

After ten minutes on the internet, I discovered Mr Reggie Terrance Porlock was a long-time resident of the Golden Shores Elderly Home. Now, I had a name and an address—a start.

The mobile phone rang. I glanced at the screen—Toby. I jabbed the answer button, my heart pounding like a drum.

"Doris, the police are keeping me here overnight."

"In a cell?"

"No, a five-star hotel suite with my own personal butler! They said they'll let me go in the morning after the medical tests on Norah's body come back. It seems she was killed by a blow to the head."

"Then you'll be free?"

"I don't know." There was an air of desperation in his voice. "The thing is...they seem to think...I did it."

I put a hand to my head. Throbbing began in my temples. "Do they have any evidence?"

"It's all so confusing," Toby muttered. "They make it sound like I was after Norah's money."

"Norah had money?" I said, straightening up, eyes staring at the phone. "How much money?"

"Oh, I don't know."

Before he'd finished the sentence, I knew he was lying. A sudden chill rose up from deep in the pit of my stomach. "Toby, are you sure?"

"Listen, I didn't kill her. Why won't anyone believe me?"

"Toby, I believe you. You know that, don't you?"

He was silent for a moment then said, "Yes."

"Norah was wealthy?"

"Doris, I don't know."

Why wasn't he giving me a straight answer? I felt a surge of frustration. "What's going on, Toby?"

There was a long silence, and I heard mumbled voices in the background. "Listen, Doris, Norah had lots of money. I don't know how much. It is in a trust fund, left by her father. He died seven years ago; her mother passed away five years before that."

"So, the police think you are after her money?"

"Yes."

That was a pretty solid motive, but it couldn't possibly be true. Toby wore his shoes until they had holes in the soles, jackets until they were threadbare. I closed my eyes grinning at that old tweed jacket he used to wear daily. "It'll last a lifetime," he had said. "It's already lasted ten years."

I shook my head, Toby was the least materialistic man I had ever met, wasn't even interested in fast cars. For an accountant, he had a remarkable disinterest in money. "The police haven't got a leg to stand on," I said with confidence.

"Why not?" His voice brightened.

"If you were after Norah's money, you'd have killed her after you were married," I said triumphantly.

"We already were," he said morosely. "We got married in a registry office two weeks ago."

I felt like I was about to throw up, gulped hard and said, "But the ceremony at the Hidden Caves Chapel—"

"Norah's idea. It was more for family and friends."

"Did you marry her for the money?" I shouted, boiling over with anger.

"Doris...I've fallen to pieces since our divorce. I'm in financial trouble...a lot of debt: gambling, drinking, drugs. That sort of thing."

I could feel the acid in my stomach bubbling up my throat, and my heart was pounding so hard I couldn't hear the individual beats. It was all I could do to contain a scream. "I'm sorry, Toby."

"Not your fault. It's my own mess..." Toby's voice trailed off, and I thought I heard a sob. "You said you loved me...then you left. Norah said she loved me...now she's dead."

"Toby, they'll need a lot more to make a case stick. Things will turn out right side up, you'll see."

"The trouble is we had an argument," Toby said in a low voice. "In the hotel lobby. I told Norah I'd had enough of Leo Warrington snooping around. I told her I had asked you to investigate him. Norah exploded with rage. I tried to explain that I'd pass anything you found to the relevant authorities—get the man put behind bars. She told me to keep my nose out, said I was interfering where I had no business. I lost my temper and said..." His voice trailed off.

"Said what?"

"Doris, believe me; it was the drink. I was in a kind of daze. And the sleeping pills, well you know all about them: makes you angry, violent."

"Toby, what did you say?"

"That I'd kill Leo Warrington. Norah slapped my face, and I threatened to kill her too—smash her face in."

"Time for a lawyer," I said softly.

"Dad has one lined up—Winston Kracho. He's travelling down from London tomorrow."

Chapter 15

AFTER I HUNG UP, I stared at the cubicle wall torn between disappointment and frustration. There was no doubt in my mind Toby was innocent, and I was to blame in part for his drinking. If I'd have stayed with him, things would have turned out differently. With a deep sense of regret I wondered who would want Norah Porlock dead, and why?

There were no obvious answers, so I returned to my notebook, my thoughts racing over all that had happened over the last few days. It wasn't long before I homed in on Leo Warrington. What did I know about him?

First, he was Norah's ex-boyfriend; second, the man's gangster style of dress suggested something outside the ordinary. "No one dresses like Bugsy Malone for a wedding," I said to the cubical wall. Then I remembered Toby had mentioned Leo was a violent thug involved in underworld crime. But what type of crime? I made a note to get more details when I next spoke with Toby.

One thing was clear, though; Leo's motive was simple—jealousy. At least a part of the puzzle had fallen into place. But that left the question of Leo's means; how did he kill Norah?

I typed *Leo Warrington* into my internet browser. It took less than five minutes to discover Leo owned an electrical wiring business. I suppressed a shiver. "Doris, you're onto something," I said once again to the cubical wall. "Perhaps the electrical blackout wasn't a random act of nature."

The question, for which I had no answer, was how did he subdue Norah and carry her body out of the chapel without being noticed? Sure, when the electricity failed, the room became pitch black. But only a minute or two passed before mobile phones flicked light into the chapel, and Norah was already gone.

"Someone locked the chapel door from the outside," I said to myself. "Norah disappeared from inside the chapel. How did Leo do it?"

"Leo who?"

I jumped.

Lucy Baxter peered over the top of my cubical wall. "Talking to yourself, eh? Not a good sign. Far better to bounce your ideas off a real person. Who are Norah and Leo?"

I took a chance and explained all I knew about Norah Porlock and Leo Warrington, being careful to exclude Toby from the conversation. I figured with Lucy's support my investigation would be easier. For once, she listened patiently without interrupting. When I was finished, she placed a hand on her cheek. "This newspaper deals with the facts. You say this Leo person dresses like a gangster and is an electrician?"

"So it seems," I replied.

"And you saw him at the wedding?"

"Yes, a very shady-looking character."

"Well, Doris, there is nothing concrete in anything I've heard; it is all circumstantial. What you need are facts. For all you know Leo might have been on his way to a fancy dress party."

Lucy was right. I felt like a rookie journalist. "Err...yes...I suppose so."

"Doris," Lucy continued, her eye's flashing with something I couldn't read, "you know better than to condemn a man because of his clothes. I was led to believe you are a seasoned journalist. I can't carry newbies on this team."

I chewed the end of my pen as she spoke. It cracked, spilling bitter tasting ink onto my tongue. "I might have got a little carried away with myself," I mumbled. "Since it is a side project, I've allowed a little more artistic licence."

"Stick to the facts. We're journalists not novel writers." Lucy's voice was hard and cold. "Porcherie Media Corporation is not in the fairy tale business. From now on, I want you to focus on the fish-and-chips-flavoured hot dogs article, that story has got legs."

So much for gaining Lucy's support, I thought, but said, "Will do."

Lucy was right about sticking to the facts, but I didn't want to admit it. Maybe it was wrong minded of me, but I needed to cling on to the hope that Toby was innocent. "The killer has to be Leo, or else..." I couldn't bear to consider that possibility, not yet.

When I was certain Lucy had returned to her office, I closed my eyes and concentrated once more on Leo. He was smoking under a tree at the entrance to the chapel when I arrived, but did I see him inside? Like an old video recorder, I ran over the images in my mind, frame by frame. I saw Mrs Lintott, the flower girls, the bridesmaids, the maid of honour, the rector, and Toby. But I didn't see Leo; then again, my focus was on the wedding party, not the guests.

"Doris, you are not a detective," I said aloud, then lowered my voice. "But you've got enough circumstantial evidence to share with Inspector Doxon, whatever Lucy Baxter thinks."

Chapter 16

A LITTLE AFTER 3 P.m. I slipped out of the *Skegness Telegraph* office, hoping no one would notice. I had two birds to kill and planned to do it with one stone. First, a meeting with Inspector Doxon. Second, go to the Golden Shores Elderly Home to visit Reggie Porlock. That would leave the evening free for my acting lessons at the community centre. The class didn't start until seven thirty.

The Skegness police station was a dull-grey concrete structure, white tile floors with pine walls and built in the nineteen seventies. At the front desk I was directed to a corner office, glass walled without windows.

"Mrs Cudlow, isn't it?" Inspector Doxon said with a look of surprise. Paperwork lay scattered across his desk along with the remains of a packet of fish and chips. "Take a seat. I'd love to offer you a coffee, but you might sue on account of the taste." He chuckled at his own joke. "How can I help you?"

"Norah Porlock's death," I said, easing into a chair.

"Oh, I thought you were here to talk about your ex-husband, Toby Cudlow." He picked up a soggy chip and popped it into his mouth. After a moment of munching, he continued,

"Mrs Cudlow, I'm not wet behind the ears. I know why you're here. Please let's not waste any more time."

"Inspector Doxon, I have information that might help apprehend Norah's killer."

He leaned back in his chair. "What makes you think the killer is not already behind bars?"

"Toby is innocent."

"Guess that's what he'll tell the judge."

"He wouldn't hurt a fly."

"Are you saying your ex-husband never raised a fist during your marriage?"

"What are you trying to say?"

"Let's not beat about the bush, Mrs Cudlow. We both know Toby is a drunk and addicted to sleeping pills. Hell, he admits that much himself. It's not much of a stretch to physical violence. For your information, we have witnesses that he threatened to kill Norah Porlock. Come now, Mrs Cudlow. He has threatened you too, in the past, hasn't he?"

"Toby was a wonderful husband. I... err... I left him for personal reasons."

Inspector Doxon picked up another chip, examined it and tossed it back into the packet. "Is that a fact? It'll do you no good to defend him. Men like Toby need to be behind bars. Now, Mrs Cudlow, you are safe here. Toby is a wife beater, isn't he?"

"No!" It was almost a scream. "Toby never laid a hand on me, never drank until after I left him."

That startled the inspector. "Well, since you're not here to cooperate," he said, regarding me with curiosity, "you've got thirty more seconds of my time. What do you want?"

"I think you should investigate a man by the name of Leo Warrington. He was Norah's ex-boyfriend—a violent man associated with the criminal underworld."

"Violent, you say?"

"Yes, extremely."

"And associated with criminal activity?"

"That's right."

The inspector leaned forward. "Do you have any proof of that?"

"No, I just—"

"I didn't think so. Look, Mrs Cudlow, I've let you take up my time because I thought you might have dirt on Toby. Any other questions before you go?" He indicated with his head towards the door.

"Just one," I said, rising to my feet. "Are you going to investigate the activities of Leo Warrington?"

"Since you asked, no." He broke into a broad grin. "Leo's firm did the rewiring on this police station. His company sponsors the annual police picnic. Mrs Cudlow, be very careful what you say about one of the outstanding members of our community."

And that was that. They let me visit with Toby in a tiny cell, but he refused to talk, saying "The room might be bugged; better wait until the morning after I've spoken with my lawyer." It hurt he was behaving this way as if he was guilty. The only glimmer of hope was that Norah was alive and in the chapel with Toby, which meant someone murdered her after she arrived for the wedding. Once the medical report determined the time of death, Toby would be in the clear. That thought lifted my spirits.

Chapter 17

THE GOLDEN SHORES ELDERLY Home was a large sprawling complex on the edge of town surrounded by green lawns and rolling hills. A cluster of small red-brick bungalows lined the entrance to a larger residential building. It had been a while since I visited an old peoples' home and expected it to be the dark and dingy place of my childhood school trips. Then, we would have to spend an afternoon each month chatting with the old-timers or singing hymns while our teacher banged out the melody on a tuneless piano.

"Reggie Porlock," I said, flashing my brightest smile. It was wasted on the receptionist as she stared into a computer screen.

"Member of his family?" she asked, glancing away from the screen and casting a curious eye in my direction.

"No," I replied, my nose twitching in delight at the pot-pourri-scented diffuser on her desk. "I'm not a relative." I didn't feel like explaining the reason for my visit.

"Reggie doesn't get many visitors. Are you from social services?"

"No."

The receptionist folded her arms across her chest and waited for an explanation. I glanced at her name tag—Siya Jones.

"Siya, I met Reggie at the wedding of Norah Porlock last Saturday."

Siya smiled. "At the Hidden Caves Chapel?"

"That's right. We were both guests at the wedding."

She shook her head, letting out a sigh. It was too long and too dramatic to be real. "Such a shame, what happened."

I thought she was talking about the death of Norah Porlock. "A tragedy and one yet to be fully resolved."

Siya looked at me with quizzical eyes. "You are from social services, aren't you? Did he write? Reggie's always writing letters. Well, his care team were very disappointed. He usually behaves himself at weddings. The rector doesn't take kindly to members of his flock running down the aisle during the matrimony service and getting up to...no good with the ladies."

"Oh, I see," I said, realizing she wasn't talking about Norah's death. "I quite understand."

"Very upsetting," she continued. "Reggie's a lady's man, likes travelling with the rector's girls. But he's been banned, at least for the rest of the spring. I'm sure he will complain to you about that, but we have our policies and procedures, and every resident must abide by the rules. There are no exceptions."

"Understood," I said in a sympathetic voice. "Totally understood. Where would our country be without rules and regulations?"

Siya nodded. "Go through to the end of the lobby; Reggie is in the sunroom."

It was like a greenhouse, huge glass windows on all sides including the roof. Reggie was wearing a white and red Skegness Town Football Association Club T-shirt, tracksuit bottoms, and black slippers. He sat still in a high-backed armchair, his eyes open, staring out into the garden.

"Reggie?" I said, slipping into a seat next to him. "Reggie Porlock?"

He didn't respond, continued staring out into the garden. He seemed ancient this close, like one of those Galapagos tortoises with a scrawny neck and bulging eyes.

"My name's Doris Cudlow," I said slowly, then spelled it out in case he was hard of hearing. "D-O-R-I-S C-U-D-L-O-W."

There was no response.

I kept talking, slow and loud. "Reggie, we met at Norah Porlock's wedding on Saturday."

"Liar!" he said, turning his ancient head, eyes glaring.

"Pardon?"

"I've never clapped eyes on you in my entire life, and please don't shout. Why you young folk like to shout at us old-timers is beyond me. Yes, I was at the wedding, but we didn't meet. Are you from social services?"

"No."

"Shame. I wrote them a letter about the treatment in this place. Thought they'd responded in person. Some hope. So who are you?"

"Doris Cudlow."

"I know that; you've already said. But we've never met."

"You're right," I said, unable to hide my surprise. "We haven't met, but I saw what happened."

"Eh?" There was a sly gleam in his eyes, and he lowered his voice. "Mrs Carter's been a widow for nigh on ten year. Can't blame a woman for seeking...a little comfort... It's all we got at our age... You her daughter or something?"

"Mrs who?"

He leaned forward in his seat. "Lady, what exactly are we talkin' about here?"

"The wedding on Saturday. I was in the congregation when the bridesmaids hustled you out of the chapel."

His face lit up with a cheeky grin. "Oh, I see. Not a relative of Mrs Carter, then?"

"No. I saw you leggin' it down the aisle on Saturday."

"You did, did you? Almost got to the front, didn't I?" He let out a little chuckle. "Ten year ago I would have made it."

"You're sprightly for a— "

"Eighty-nine-year-old," he said finishing my sentence. "And I intend to live to one hundred. Now, Doris, what do you want?"

"To see how you're doing."

"Horse poop."

"Eh?"

"I may be old, but I'm not senile. First, we have never met. Second, you didn't come out here from wherever you live to pass the time of day. Can we drop the horse poop and get to the action?"

"I thought they brought your generation up with manners," I said in a startled voice.

He glanced at me curiously and shrugged. "We were, but I'm stuck here all day in front of daytime television; that changes a man. What's that black stuff around your mouth; you work as a clown in your day job?"

I wiped my mouth and peered at my hand to see smudges of black ink. I couldn't help myself and burst out laughing. "Chewed my pen earlier today! Okay, I'll cut the horse poop. I saw you at the wedding of Norah Porlock, and you said she was your wife."

"Oh, did I? Well... I... err... I was in a hurry, stumbled over my words. It happens at my age. What I meant to say was—"

"Reggie, dear, time for your evening medication." The voice came from an oversized nurse who bustled into the room, injected something into Reggie's arm, and disappeared as quickly as she had appeared.

"Go on, Reggie; you were saying," I said when she left.

Reggie's head slumped to one side, a smile on his face, but his eyes were closed, and he was snoring.

"You won't get any sense out of him now, dear," said an elderly woman in a wheelchair a few feet away. "Once he's had his night-time shot, he is out for the count. Wish they'd give me some of that snooze juice, but that's reserved for the over eighties. You'd think we seventy-eight-year olds don't have difficulty sleeping."

Chapter 18

"TONIGHT, WE'LL DISCUSS the importance of staying in character," said Natalie Nordstrom, the Skegness Community Centre acting coach. I had arrived at the class just as it was about to start, having learned little from Reggie Porlock. I'd planned to visit with him again; this time earlier in the day and well before his night-time shot of snooze juice.

"This evening we'll spend the last half an hour in the presence of a surprise guest," Natalie boomed in her sing-song New York accent, half turning towards a small room at the back of the class. Through the glass panel of the door a silhouette raised a hand and waved. I waved back, but it was impossible to make out whether the individual was a man or woman.

"Now," Natalie continued, "is everyone ready to play their part in tonight's class?"

"Yes," we roared, all four of us. The class officially enrolled twenty-five, but only Janet, Annabelle, and Pete showed up week in, week out. Annabelle and Pete Brown were a retired couple. Janet was their five-year-old granddaughter. Tuesday evenings they babysit Janet, and rather than stay in their council house they brought the child to the acting class.

"Doris, can you step forward please?"

"Hey, what about us?" Pete grumbled. "Why does Doris always get first dibs?"

"Don't worry, everyone will get a turn," Natalie replied, waving me to the front of the class.

Pete gave a sigh of resignation. "I'll never get to Hollywood at this rate!"

Natalie placed her hands on her hips and rolled her eyes. "Pete, you're up next, okay?"

"I don't want to go next, not now. I saw your eye movements. The council said this course was for all comers. It mentioned nothing about the instructor rolling her eyes cynically at the students. It's very off-putting."

"Quite right, Pete," chimed in Annabelle," and what with the council taxes so high and all. To think the people of Skegness are paying through the nose for the instructor to stand at the front of the class and roll her eyes at students. It's a ruddy scandal!"

"Grandad," said Janet, tugging on Pete's arm. "Can I go with you to Hollywood to see Mickey Mouse?"

"Of course you can, darling," Pete said, looking down at his granddaughter. "When me and Grandma break into the movies, we'll fly you first class to California to stay with us in our palace."

"And Miss Natalie too?" Janet let go of Pete's arm and ran to give the class instructor a hug. "I want Miss Natalie to go with me."

Pete rolled his eyes. "Of course, darling. Miss Natalie Nordstrom, Donald Duck, and your special blanket. We'll fly them out with you, first class."

"Love you, Granddad."

"Are we ready?" Natalie said, clapping her hands.

There was a general murmur of agreement.

"Staying in role is one of the key characteristics to acting success," she said. "That one skill got me into television commercials, radio shows, even a bit part on Broadway, and now it fuels my passion, sharing what I know to help others achieve their acting dreams."

"From New York to Skegness," Annabelle said. "Seems like you're going in the wrong direction there, love."

Natalie ignored the comment and continued, "Doris, here's the scenario. I want you to imagine your husband has been wrongly accused of a crime, arrested and thrown in the slammer. What emotions does that evoke?"

I couldn't help myself. It had been a difficult day. I burst out crying.

"That's it!" Natalie said in an excited voice. "That's what I want to see."

Tears streamed down my eyes, snot from my nose, and I was trembling.

"Raw emotion is like raw sewage—it stinks," Natalie cooed, full of confidence and clapping her hands in excitement. "But without it the city is full of..." She looked down at little Janet who stared back, eyes wide and eager."Well, the same goes for emotionless acting."

I fell to the floor, kicking and screaming.

"Wonderful," Natalie said, her voice not quite as confident. "But you can stop now."

But I couldn't.

I was sobbing uncontrollably, rolling around, mumbling. "It's not fair... It's all my fault... I wish I could turn back the clock...but it's too late."

"Oh my," Annabelle cried. "Doris, you're so realistic. It brings a tear to my own eyes."

"Mine too," added Pete. "Maybe Doris should teach the class instead of Miss New York."

After three minutes, somehow, I regained control, wiped my nose with my sleeve, breathed in deeply, and exhaled. "I'm okay, now," I said in a weak voice. "Feel much better."

"Bravo," Natalie said. "The mumbling was a little over the top, otherwise you played it perfect." Again, she clapped her hands. "Now, everyone try."

For the next twenty minutes, individually and in our small group, we bawled our eyes out. Each time using a different scenario—the loss of a loved one, sudden diagnosis of a terminal illness, and at Janet's insistence, losing our favourite toy when we were three. I felt light and cheerful at the end of that exercise.

"Now we go to the plains of Africa, in our imagination, of course," Natalie said, striding to the front of the class. "How many of you saw the movie *Born Free*? It's about lions who roam the African savannah."

"Kenya," interrupted Pete. "They set the movie in Kenya."

"And it's about Elsa the lioness, an orphaned lion cub," chimed in Annabelle. "Do you know who starred in the 1966 movie, Natalie?"

"That's too easy," Janet squeaked. "Virginia McKenna as Joy Adamson, and Bill Travers as George Adamson. See, it was too easy for Miss Natalie!"

"Superb," Natalie responded, eyes darting around nervously. "No more questions because tonight we will sense what it feels like to be a lioness on the African plains. Follow me." She trotted at a steady pace around the edge of the hall. We fell into line behind. "Imagine you are prowling for food under a blazing African sun."

"Lions hunt at night when it's cooler, actually," Pete moaned.

"In Hollywood anything is possible," Natalie replied and crouched low.

We followed.

"Now, you see a hunter with a big ole gun. What would you do?" She held up her hand. "Run like Elsa." She huffed picking up the pace.

I'm not fit or athletic; my only exercise is walking up and down the stairs at the boarding house. It wasn't long before running like Elsa left me gasping for breath.

"Keep running," Natalie urged. "You are a lioness, queen of the jungle, chasing gazelle on the African savannah!"

Finally, Natalie clapped her hands, and the exercise was over.

"Cor blimey!" Pete said, gasping for breath, "I'd rather watch it on the telly."

"Now." Natalie puffed as a trickle of sweat ran down her forehead. "I would like to introduce our surprise guest." She walked to a door at the back of the room, stuck her head in and said, "We'll be ready for you in a moment." Then she returned to the centre of the room.

"Our guest tonight will talk about how to stay in role during our day-to-day lives. This is an essential skill to master as it allows you to better portray characters on the stage. Ladies and gentlemen, please join me in welcoming one of the Skegness Player's greatest contemporary actors, Mr Leo Warrington."

Chapter 19

THE DOOR TO THE SMALL room creaked open, and Leo Warrington stepped into our classroom. He wore the same dark-navy-blue, pinstripe suit and black-and-white shoes as he had at the wedding, but pulled the fedora down casting a shadow over his eyes. In his right hand, he held a roll-up cigarette, in his left a small black handgun which he jabbed jerkily in the air as he sauntered to the front of the room.

"Ladies and gentlemen," he began, pointing the gun at Natalie, "Your personal teaching coach asked me to make a small presentation on one of the most important aspects of the professional actor—staying in role."

He slipped the handgun into his jacket pocket, crushed the cigarette, then tossed it into a dustbin. "Staying in role can seem extreme to those who are not actors. I'm playing 'Moonface' Martin in the Lincoln Playhouse's production of *Anything Goes*. That's why, for three months, I've dressed as a gangster and carried this toy gun. It's caused no end of speculation here in town, but a good actor doesn't explain. Anyone know why?"

Pete raised his hand. "Because it breaks the role," he said with triumph.

"Exactly! And once you are out of role, it's difficult to get back in."

"A sage bit of advice," Natalie chimed in, her eyes smiling at Leo.

Leo surveyed the gathered faces. "In my day job, I run an electrical wiring company. We did this community centre, ten years back." He waved his arms around the room. "So, you can imagine with employees and ongoing contracts, it is difficult, but I managed it. I've stayed in role. And I'll do so until opening night on Saturday the twenty-first. Questions?"

Annabelle raised her hand. "I'm auditioning for the role of a munchkin in the Skegness Players production of *Charlie and the Chocolate Factory*. I really want to get the part. How long should I stay in role to guarantee they'll pick me?"

Leo placed his hands on his hips as if contemplating the question, then smiled. "You sure you want the role?"

"Yes."

"Then stay in role for as long as it takes to get the role."

"That's brilliant advice, Mr Warrington," Natalie said emphatically. "Class, I hope you are taking notes. Don't miss these nuggets of pure solid gold."

"But what on earth does it mean?" grumbled Pete. "Are we talking two weeks or two years here?"

"Until you think like the character, see like the character, and feel like the character," Leo said excited, eyes sparkling. Like a hound on a scent, he continued, "Only once you have those three in place, will you be the character you wish to portray. Then, and only then, will the role be yours."

"So, my wife has to become a munchkin. Is that what you are saying?" replied Pete acidly.

Leo prowled jerkily around the room. "To be 'Moonface' Martin, I've had to become 'Moonface' Martin." He continued his low gangster-style prowl. "See what I mean?"

"Oh yes, I see," said Annabelle with enthusiasm and turned to Pete. "From now on I'm a munchkin."

"Excellent," Natalie said, clapping her hands. "Leo, this has been very helpful. Before we wrap up, are there any other questions?"

"Yes," I said, raising a hand and thinking fast. "Leo, I saw you at the Hidden Caves Chapel on Saturday, dressed as a gangster, and I wondered—"

"You were at the wedding?" His face suddenly crumpled into a scowl.

"Yes, a guest of the groom."

For several moments he stood still, mouth agape, then said. "What do you do for a living Miss...?"

"Mrs Cudlow. I'm a reporter for the *Skegness Telegraph*."

If I hadn't been watching closely, I would have missed it—a startled flash in his eyes. It was only momentary, but it was there. He folded his arms across his chest. "Such a shame what happened. I didn't know the couple, but my company rewired the chapel three months ago. I oversaw the project. Don't like to brag, but we did a wonderful job, if I say so myself. What did you think of the candlelight effect?"

"Gave it a mysterious aura," I said, then added, "I was in the chapel when the lights went out."

A sheen of perspiration formed on Leo's forehead. "Happens sometimes. It must have been dark in there without the lights, eh?"

"So, you were outside the chapel when the lights went out?"

Leo was perspiring heavily. "I... err... Ladies and gentlemen, we are getting a little off track here. Are there any more questions about staying in role?" He spoke in a cheery voice, although there was a hint of alarm in his eyes.

There were no further questions.

"That's a wrap," Natalie said, once again clapping her hands. "See everyone next Tuesday."

Typically, I leave when the lesson is over. But tonight, I made straight for Leo Warrington. He had retreated to the small room at the back of the class and stood behind a desk packing his fedora into a bag.

"Leo," I said as he gathered up his things. "I'm looking into the death of Norah Porlock. You said you didn't know the couple. I thought you were Norah's ex-boyfriend."

He drew a sharp breath through pursed lips. "What makes you think that?"

"I'm a reporter. I have my sources."

Leo turned away, his face in profile. "Such a tragedy. I hear they have Norah's husband in custody." His voice was slow and careful.

"Where were you when the chapel lights went out?" I asked, not holding back.

"I hear," Leo said slowly and turned back to face me, "they found Norah's body on the beach, face half eaten by crabs. Not a nice way for a young lady to end up, is it?"

I countered with a question. "Were you outside the chapel when the lights went out?"

"Norah's husband will be in for a long stretch behind bars," he said with a certain satisfaction.

"Strange," I said.

"What is?" asked Leo.

"Twice now you've referred to Norah's husband. How did you know they were married?"

He blinked. "I misspoke." He blinked again. "I meant to say her fiancé."

I placed my hand on the desk partly to steady myself, partly to gather my thoughts. "If you didn't know the couple, why were you at the wedding?"

No answer.

"It won't take the police long to figure out Norah disappeared when the lights went out."

Leo rubbed his chin with the back of his hand but said nothing.

"Since you're the electrician," I continued, "I guess they'll be asking you a few questions. What are you going to tell Inspector Doxon?"

His hand flew to his collar, and he tugged hard to loosen it. "What are you trying to say?"

I took a chance, knew it was wild speculation even before I'd finished speaking. "Someone tampered with the electrical wiring and caused a power outage during the wedding service. Then Norah disappears...washed up dead on a beach."

Leo was perspiring freely, damp patches of moisture visible through his collar. His hand reached into the bag, and he took out the fedora, placed it on his head and pulled it down over his eyes. Then he paced the room with one hand behind his back as if he were thinking of a solution to a difficult puzzle.

At last he said, "What else do you know?" His eyes were hidden by the brim of his hat, but I knew they were staring at me, hard.

"Everything." It wasn't true, but I wanted to spook him. "Leo, I met with Inspector Doxon this evening. I've shared some of my findings, but not all yet. Not until I've spoken with you."

Natalie hurried into the room. "The community centre is closing in ten minutes. Where are you taking me for dinner, Leo?" She paused, glanced at Leo, then back at me. "Is everything okay? Leo, you're sweating; are you feeling well?"

"I'm fine," Leo replied, then turned to face me, lowering his voice to a whisper. "Listen, I can't talk now. Can you meet me at the Fiddlers Bowl Café tomorrow at noon? I'll get a seat by the window."

Chapter 20

LATER THAT NIGHT, IN the stillness of my tiny bedsitter room, I lay on my bed staring at the ceiling, deep in thought. The open curtains let in the street light; the shadows drew strange pictures on the bedroom wall. At one moment they took the form of Leo Warrington, in another a bride in a flowing gown, and yet another as a swirling mist. Eventually I drifted into sleep, but my rest was filled with a vivid, intense dream.

I was in the lobby of the *Skegness Telegraph*, stepping through the doorway in a hurry to share my findings with Lucy Baxter, but the newsroom went on and on, filled with a neverending sequence of cubicles scattered haphazardly like a cornfield maze. I struggled to find my way through, becoming disorientated after twisting and turning from one dead end after another.

"Help! Please help," a voice called from Lucy's office. "Hurry!"

At one final turn, I could see light shining through Lucy's office door. I hurried faster. "Hello! I'm coming," I called in my sleep. "Don't worry, I'm on the way."

"In here," called the voice again. "Please hurry."

I was at the door now, tugging at the handle. It was locked. Panting, out of breath I grasped the handle with both hands and pulled with a superhuman effort. The door swung open. An alarm sounded.

Brrring, brrring, brrring.

Instinctively I sat up.

"Hello," I said into the mobile phone, my voice filled with sleep. "Who is it?"

"Doris, it's Toby. Guess what? I'm free! Winston Kracho, my lawyer, completed the paperwork. I'm out!"

"Free?" I said dreamily, consciousness slowly returning.

"Doris, are you awake? They have released me from the police station. Can't leave town, though. Inspector Doxon wasn't happy, but he can't just throw a person into a police cell and keep them there without charges."

"What did the inspector say?" I was awake now and glanced at the bedside clock—9 a.m.

"Doxon said he'd have me back behind bars before the week was out." Toby let out a chuckle. His words slurred. "That'll never happen. They won't take me alive."

"Toby, have you been drinking?" I couldn't hide the anxiety in my voice.

"There's not much to do in a police cell but think and wait. Been thinking a lot...about Leo Warrington...and waiting." He was breathing hard.

"Where are you?"

"Free. That's all you need to know, honey."

"Toby, please tell me where you are. I want to help."

"I should have done this right from the start; now Norah is dead, it doesn't matter." Toby's voice was harsh, filled with an emotion I hadn't thought him capable of—hatred.

"Toby, what are you talking about?"

"Doris, I've got a score to settle...with Leo Warrington, and I mean to do it today."

Chapter 21

"TOBY!"

The line went dead.

He sounded drunk, or on drugs, or both. I knew what that was like, knew his rational mind was at the mercy of his instincts. What if he went through with his threat, tracked Leo down and then what? I shuddered at the thought but relaxed at another—Toby wasn't a violent man. He barely raised his voice in our marriage, was slow to anger, and never held a grudge for long. The Toby I knew was the last person on earth who would get into an altercation with Leo Warrington, or anyone else.

I glanced at the bedside clock. "Nine ten!" I tumbled out of bed and sprinted towards the bathroom. "I'm going to be late again; Oh bugger!"

Thud, thud, thud.

"Sorry, Mr Pandy. I'm late for work."

Thud, thud, thud.

In the shower I thought about Toby, Norah, and Leo. Drink changes a person, as do drugs. At the back of my mind an unwanted thought niggled—could Toby have changed so much he..."No!" I said as the steamy water splashed over my face. After my lunchtime meeting with Leo Warrington, things would become a little clearer—or at least that's what I hoped. Then I thought about the *Skegness Telegraph*. If I survived until tomorrow, I'd be on the newspaper's permanent payroll. I dashed out of the shower.

Thud, thud, thud.

The clock behind the security desk at the *Skegness Telegraph* said nine forty-five as I bustled into the newsroom. I turned around the corner and darted straight for my cubicle. I kept my head hung low, scurrying as I did in my dream, not wanting to draw any attention. Tomorrow I'd be a member of the permanent staff and could relax a little; if they fired me, I'd be entitled to three months' redundancy pay.

In the narrow passageway that led to my workspace I let out a sigh then gasped in horror.

Lucy Baxter stood in my cubicle, arms crossed.

She wasn't smiling.

"Just arrived?" she said, somehow filling the space of the tiny cubical with a sour aura.

I squinted, staring at her face trying to determine how to respond. At last, I said, "Late night last night, overslept."

"Punctuality and timeliness are critical for success in the news media business, I'm sure you appreciate that?" Her voice was slow and stilted as if she was thinking about something else as she spoke.

Choosing an excuse in the hope it would ease the situation, I said, "Sorry, I got sidetracked with the side project for the newspaper. It won't happen again." Then, wondering what she wanted, I asked, "You were looking for me; how can I help you?"

"Oh, nothing," she said with a flick of her hand. "Have you spoken to Mr Hornsby about his hot dogs?"

"Top of my list for this morning," I said, sounding chirpier than I felt. "I'll call him in a moment."

Her eyes narrowed. "Does that mean the side project you worked on last night wasn't to do with fish-and-chip-flavoured hot dogs?" She turned, hustled away before I answered.

I let out a breath I didn't realize I'd been holding, slumped in my chair, picked up the desk phone, and dialed.

"Mr Hornsby?"

"Yeah, what do you want?" replied a gruff voice.

"Doris Cudlow from the *Skegness Telegraph*. I'm writing a feature on your fish-and-chip-flavoured hot dogs. Is now a good time to talk?"

Chapter 22

IT WAS A LITTLE BEFORE 11 a.m. when I heard the official-sounding voices. They pried their way into the edges of my consciousness as I reviewed my notes from the call with Mr Hornsby. If I weren't so tired, I would have paid greater attention. However, groggy and worried over Toby, I ignored the voices until it was too late.

"Mrs Doris Cudlow?"

Inspector Doxon stood at the cubical entrance, his face as stern as a schoolmaster.

I looked up, heart skipping a beat. At the inspector's side, Constable Wriggly, who fidgeted with his hat, eyes darting around. My mouth went dry. "Inspector Doxon, what is—"

The inspector raised a finger to his lips as if he was about to whisper but continued in his normal voice. "Rather bad news, I'm afraid. We've discovered a body, need you for identification."

"Toby!" I said in a startled voice, almost a scream. "You've found Toby." It was more of a statement than a question.

Inspector Doxon turned, his face shielded from my eyes. "I'm sorry, Mrs Cudlow. Please take a moment to gather your things. Constable Wriggly will wait for you here. I'll be in the car park."

My heart was thumping, and I was panting slightly. "Please God, no!" This must be what hell feels like, I thought, as numbness washed over my body.

"Mrs Cudlow, take your time; there's no hurry, now," said Officer Wriggly, almost too softly to be heard above my pounding heart. "The body won't be going anywhere."

The thought of Toby lying on the cold hard mortician's slab sent a stabbing wave of pain through my body, but instinct took over as I picked up my things—keys, bag, purse. Other co-workers gathered around, peering over the cubical wall, eyes wide like curious cattle, voices whispering in a low sympathetic murmur.

Then I heard Lucy Baxter's voice.

"What's going on?" she asked, shoving through the gathered crowd.

I thought back to all my journalism training and acting classes and tried to keep it together. But my voice cracked as I spoke: "Inspector Doxon has asked for my help to identify a body."

Her eyes grew wide. "Why you?"

I shook my head, voice dropped to a whisper. "I believe it is Toby Cudlow, my ex-husband."

Lucy's mouth curved in mock sympathy, but her eyes expressed something else—shock. "Toby Cudlow was your husband?" She was unable to hide the surprise in her voice. "And he's dead?"

I was already walking towards the exit and didn't answer. Lucy hurried after. In the lobby, she touched my arm with a cold, clammy hand.

"I'm sorry, Doris," she said in a low voice as if she didn't want anyone to hear.

"Thank you," I replied without glancing in her direction.

"No, Doris, I don't think you understand." There was a harshness to her voice. "I'm letting you go. Since you're not a member of the permanent staff, you're not entitled to redundancy pay. However, I'll ensure you are paid for today. The security guard will box up your cubicle and deliver the contents to your home address. I'm sorry it didn't work out. Please don't ever come back."

Chapter 23

IT WAS AWFUL.

The mortuary was in the basement of Skegness General Hospital—white tile walls, polished concrete floor, cold, clinical, air heavy with the scent of disinfectant and death. The mortuary attendant, a thin, wiry man, who had been dozing at his desk, jumped up on our approach.

"Inspector Doxon, this way, please," he said without giving eye contact and disappearing into a room behind his desk. Conduits and ducts ran across the ceiling, and little stainless-steel doors lined the walls. They reminded me of the firebox door on a steam locomotive. Constable Wriggly hung back by the entrance.

"Come on, Wriggly," barked Inspector Doxon. Then, as Officer Wriggly hesitantly walked into the room, the inspector touched my arm, eyes hard, as if he'd seen it all before. "Are you ready, Mrs Cudlow?"

I clenched my jaw, fought back the acid bubbling in my stomach. "Yes," I said, not knowing how the words came out. "I'm ready."

Inspector Doxon nodded at the mortician. With a flourish reminiscent of a magician on the stage, he reached out a hand, hesitated for a moment over one of the silver doors, then pressed the handle and pulled it open.

A tray slid out silently.

I clenched my fists, head dizzy, unable to think or process anything as I stared at the thin green sheet covering the body. That Lucy Baxter had fired me on my way to identify the corpse of my dead ex-husband hadn't registered yet. That I was out of work, again, didn't feel real. Even though I was physically in the hospital basement surrounded by death, I felt as if I was in a dream, and at any moment I might wake up.

I waited for this nightmare to pass.

Inspector Doxon's voice brought reality flooding back. "Mrs Cudlow, are you ready?"

I couldn't take my eyes off the covered body and nodded mutely.

"Remove the sheet," Inspector Doxon ordered.

The room vanished. Only the thin hand of the mortician hovering over the sheet and the body hidden underneath remained. With another flourish, the mortician yanked off the cover.

Dull blue eyes stared vacantly towards the ceiling. The side of the head battered and bruised.

"It's not Toby," I said in a hoarse whisper.

"No," Inspector Doxon agreed. "But you know who it is, don't you?"

"Yes," I whispered. "Leo Warrington."

Chapter 24

"YOU KNEW IT WASN'T Toby," I said, barely able to contain my fury. "You knew the corpse was Leo Warrington!"

We were sitting in the hospital cafeteria. The clatter of plates, low mumble of voices, and the savoury smells of lunch were a welcome relief from the stale air of the mortuary. Constable Wriggly had disappeared with instructions to bring three mugs of tea.

Inspector Doxon took a long breath, letting the air curl out slowly from between his teeth. "Mrs Cudlow, a hotel worker found the body this morning in Suite 654 of the Silver Beach Hotel." He paused, watching my face closely. "Does that mean anything to you?"

"No," I said, my mind racing.

"Are you quite sure of that, Mrs Cudlow?"

"Yes."

Tiny frown lines creased his forehead. Someone dropped a tray; the plates clattered with a sharp thud, followed by mumbled voices. "Have you ever visited the Silver Beach Hotel?"

"Why are you asking me this? I've never been to that hotel. Is it here in Skegness?"

"Yes, Mrs Cudlow; the hotel is here in town. It is the hotel your ex-husband, Toby Cudlow, was staying in. Suite 654 was his room."

I glanced at the hard eyes of Inspector Doxon and felt a disquieting sensation in the pit of my stomach, followed by dizziness. "You can't seriously—"

The inspector raised his hand. "Mrs Cudlow, you're a journalist, and deal in facts. Isn't that correct?" He didn't wait for an answer. "The fact is Toby Cudlow killed Norah Porlock. Why? So he could get his grubby hands on her trust fund. I suspect he needed the money to fund his drink and drug habits and pay off gambling debts."

"Tea's up," said Officer Wriggly, placing three mugs of milky tea on the table and a plate of sausage rolls. "Sup up, Mrs Cudlow. It'll bring the colour back to your face. Things always seem brighter after a good cuppa and a sausage roll."

I took a sip, mainly to give myself time to think, to process what I'd heard. Toby had said he was in financial debt, had a drink and drugs problem, had things to settle with Leo Warrington. But murder?

"The facts speak for themselves, Mrs Cudlow," the inspector continued. "Mrs Symons, the cleaner, found the body of Leo Warrington in your husband's hotel room." He gave me a long, resigned look. "I think you'll agree; we have all the facts we need."

I took a deep breath to fight back the nausea bubbling up in my stomach. "But there has to be an alternative explanation—" My voice wavered, flooded with confusion. "Toby's not a—"

"Murderer," interrupted the inspector, speaking slowly and picking his words carefully, "I'm afraid Toby is in rather serious trouble...and has disappeared, gone into hiding, if you will."

"Do yourself a favour," chipped in Officer Wriggly. "Take another sip of tea and maybe a bite or two of that sausage roll, and tell us what you know. The monster needs to be behind bars. It'll be for the best."

Inspector Doxon placed a hand on my shoulder and smiled but there was no humour in it. "Now, are you ready?"

"I... I... err..."

"Now, Mrs Cudlow, the time to protect your ex-husband has passed. It's time to tell the truth."

It was all so depressing. My rational mind confessed what the rest of me couldn't, not yet—everything pointed to Toby. "No!" I said with defiance. "Toby is not the killer." I stood up.

Inspector Doxon's face crimsoned, his eyes shrunk to black dots. "Sit down!" His voice cracked like a whip.

I sat.

"Drugs and drink can change a man," he said, his voice softening slightly. He leaned forward over the table. "Where is he, Mrs Cudlow; where is Toby?"

Chapter 25

I WALKED ALONE ON THE sandy beach, wind to my back, occasionally glancing out to sea at the wind turbines off in the distance. Heaps of gleaming seaweed were strewn about the shore like a matted rug. Bits of driftwood, broken shells, pebbles, and a few skeletons of half-eaten fish lay where the tide had deposited them.

I wasn't sure whether Inspector Doxon believed I didn't know Toby's whereabouts. He'd sighed and waved me out of his presence when he realized there was little I would tell him. "If Toby attempts to make contact," he had said, cold eyes flashing like steel, "call us."

The blustery wind intensified the tang of salt and seaweed while the rhythmic sound of the waves crashing against the shore reminded me of the regularity of a pendulum swing in a grandfather clock as it marked the passage of time. I wouldn't let myself believe Toby was responsible, not even drunk and drug-crazed. There had to be another explanation, but what?

I was heading towards the Hidden Caves Chapel, mind racing but no single thought took hold for long, and I felt as if my feet were trapped in sinking sand. I'd lost my job, identified a corpse, had my ex-husband accused of two murders, and the police were convinced I knew his hideout. Life had turned everything on its head.

The sun peeked through the clouds, and I felt its watery rays on the back of my neck. For an instant, the world had gone silent and all I could hear was my breathing, footsteps, and the distant cries of faraway seagulls. At that moment all my fears raised their heads. Suppose it is true, I thought. Suppose Toby is the murderer? What if I'm wrong? I felt a sudden pressure in my chest as if my heart had turned to iron and was being pulled by a magnet.

"If Toby killed Norah and Leo, then, in part, I'm to blame."

I stopped, realizing I was beneath the Hidden Caves Chapel. A rocky staircase cut into the hillside snaked up to the building. For several minutes my eyes traced the uneven steps to the top. It wasn't an easy climb, but in a wedding dress, under a greying April sky, it seemed impossible. Yet, Norah Porlock's body was found on the beach, not too far from here.

"The explanation," I said aloud, "is simple. Someone killed Norah elsewhere and dumped the body on the beach."

The question for which I had no answer was who?

For several moments I mused on Leo Warrington. Suppose, somehow, he snatched Norah from the church during the blackout. But he wouldn't have been able to do that on his own. He'd have needed help. I closed my eyes and leaned into the breeze, replaying the images of the wedding in my mind. What did I see outside the chapel? What did I see inside? Was anyone acting unusual?

Then I saw it. The two men standing by the ambulance as I hurried with Mrs Lintott to the chapel entrance. They stared at the doorway as if waiting for something—a signal, perhaps? I thought there was something unusual, but now in the fresh sea breeze, it became clear. Leo worked with these two men. They grabbed Norah in the darkness and bustled her into the ambulance.

"Yes, that's it!" I shouted, remembering the sound of the siren racing away as the chapel filled with darkness. "I've figured it out, cracked the case."

I whirled around, headed back in the direction from which I came, at a fast clip. As I walked, I talked out loud, the wind blowing my words back and forth like a ping pong ball.

"But why did Leo snatch her at the wedding?

"Because he was a jealous ex-boyfriend.

"No, no, that can't be right. For one thing, Leo could have made a scene at the altar. Second, he had an invitation. Third, Leo was a prominent businessman. Fourth, he was a ham actor. Fifth...

"Okay, Clever Clogs, so why did he kidnap Norah at the wedding?"

It was hard work walking into the wind. I slowed my pace a little. I continued talking to myself.

"Why does anyone commit a crime?

"Passion or money or both.

"Money! The trust funds."

I saw it all now with poisonous clarity. Norah had been kidnapped, and something had gone wrong.

"They didn't pay the ransom."

I trudged up the narrow gravel path that led from the beach to the car park, elated. It all made sense now...except for two things. First, Toby hadn't mentioned a ransom note, nor had Inspector Doxon. Second, Leo was dead.

The wind picked up, stirring sand and dead leaves around my feet. "Third, what was Leo doing in Toby's hotel room?" I was at the door of the Micra. The sense of elation gone.

As I climbed into the car, I realized what had seemed clear on the beach was little more than a wild jumble of baseless speculation. Now, as I stared out of the windscreen, the truth stared me in the face. I didn't know who killed Leo Warrington; I had no idea who murdered Norah Porlock, but I admitted to myself in the blustery salt-filled air, the most likely candidate was Toby Cudlow.

Chapter 26

IT WAS AFTER I WAS back in my bedsit that I felt the weight of the day most keenly. I'd taken a shower to warm myself up, but the room felt cold and empty. "I need a drink," I said as I sat at the kitchen table. "After a day like today, I deserve it."

I kept several cans of beer in the fridge, and a half-empty bottle of gin in the cupboard above the sink. The Alcoholics Anonymous counsellor advised me to get rid of them. "Don't put yourself in the way of temptation," he had said. But I kept the cans and bottle anyway. They'd been with me for months, untouched: so had the pills in the medicine cabinet.

"Try to keep busy," the counsellor had said. "If you lead an active life, you minimize the risk of falling back into the pit."

I looked around the tiny room. A pile of dirty dishes in the sink, a stack of unwashed clothes in the corner, and piles of books and yellowing magazines I hadn't yet read.

"You're right," I said to the counsellor, knowing he couldn't hear me, wasn't even in the room. "I've got to keep busy."

With gusto, I tidied up. The clothes were dropped into a laundry bag and placed by the door ready for my next visit to the laundromat; the books and magazines were sorted through and stacked neatly, then the dishes.

It didn't take long.

Once again, I was alone with my thoughts.

I fired up my laptop, peered into the screen and got busy. After I had checked my email, social media, and glanced at the six o'clock news, I wandered over to the fridge, snapped a can from the six-pack and sat at the kitchen table. There was no work to go to in the morning, nothing to get up early for. I hoped Toby would call, but I didn't expect it.

I cracked open a beer can.

Knock, knock, knock.

"Yoo hoo! Doris, are you in there?" It was Mrs Lintott.

"Door's open. Come in."

Mrs Lintott bustled into the room carrying a tray with two large plates, each covered by a stainless-steel domed lid. "I heard what happened; thought I'd bring you dinner," she said, placing the tray on the kitchen table and carefully lifting out one plate.

"Bad-hair day," I muttered. I wasn't certain which of the many things she was referring to. "What have you heard?"

"Everything." She sat down in a chair opposite.

"But—"

"The postie saw you walking along a deserted stretch of beach earlier. Said you were looking out at the wind turbines, all alone, and in that stiff breeze too!"

"I suppose he took bets on whether I would run into the sea."

Mrs Lintott smiled. "Darling, Mrs Symons cleans the Hidden Caves Chapel. She also saw you on the beach. You gave her quite a fright standing on the sand staring up towards the chapel, especially given she'd discovered the body of Leo Warrington earlier..." She stopped talking for a moment and placed a hand on her cheek. "Things will seem a little brighter once you have eaten something." She nodded towards the plate and added, "There is always another job, you know."

"You know about me losing my job?" I said astonished.

"And that you were at the hospital...in the morgue...and your ex-husband is on the run..."

"So, I guess you know everything," I said with a heavy sigh.

"Don't be daft; I'm not a clairvoyant. Two people spotted you on the beach, that's all; Constable Wriggly will do anything for a sausage roll, and I know Winston Holmes, the mortician—a thin, wiry man, with his nose always in the newspaper." She paused, eyeing me with concern. "I hope you aren't thinking of doing anything rash?"

I stretched my hand towards the can, put it to my lips. The hoppy smell excited my taste buds. If only I could stop at one. "No," I said, putting the can down. "I don't think so."

"Good, because there is one thing I know about Toby Cudlow," Mrs Lintott said with a faint smile.

"What's that?"

"You still love him, don't you?"

I got up from the table and moved restlessly about the room, trying not to answer her question. At last, I sat back down. "Yes," I admitted, avoiding her eyes. "I do."

"Then why did you two split up?"

"My problem," I said, tapping the side of my head. "I was spiralling out of control."

"Drink?"

I nodded.

"And pills too?"

I stared at Mrs Lintott. "How did you know?"

"I'm clairvoyant."

"What?"

"Had you there, didn't I?" She chuckled.

"Very funny!"

"Skegness is a small town; news gets around." Mrs Lintott pushed the can of beer out of my reach. "You need to get proper food into your stomach; fermented hops just won't cut it."

She lifted off the silver cover. "Homemade steak and kidney pudding, boiled potatoes tossed in garlic butter, and string beans. An old recipe reserved for days like this. Goes well with a glass of water."

The savoury smell stirred hunger pangs in my stomach. "Thank you," I said, close to tears. "Didn't think I could eat a bite, but now I realize I'm starving."

Mrs Lintott stood up. Picked up the tray with the remaining plate and walked towards the door. "Take my advice, love. Ditch the beer; it does nothing for a lady like you."

Chapter 27

I COULD TELL BY THE slant of sunlight shining through the bedroom window it was late. The bedside clock said 10 a.m. My head pounded like a bass drum. "No," I said to the empty room. "Not getting up till noon."

I turned over, body stiff and achy, pulling the sheet over my head. I felt like I'd been drinking all night. My joints were sore from the walk along the beach. My mind hurt over the death of Norah Porlock, losing my job, and one hundred and one other things. But at least I wasn't hung-over, hadn't touched a drop—one point for me.

The mobile phone chirped as I attempted to drift back to sleep. "Toby," I said aloud but felt a surge of disappointment when I didn't recognize the number. "Hello, who is it?"

"Is this the actress, Mrs Doris Cudlow?" The voice was high-pitched and squeaky.

"I don't think anyone's called me that before."

"Am I speaking to Doris?" The voice sounded weird, almost like that of a ventriloquist dummy.

"Who is this?"

"I heard about Leo Warrington, Norah Porlock, and your ex-husband, Toby Cudlow."

That got my full interest. Rubbing the sleep from my eyes, I said, "Do you have any information about who committed the murders?"

There was an audible gasp. "Don't you know who this is?"

"Whoever you are, you've got my attention. What do you want?"

There was a long silence followed by another gasp. "I can't believe it's working!"

Then it struck me. "Annabelle! Why are you speaking in that strange voice?"

"I had you fooled for a moment, didn't I?" Her voice remained unusually high-pitched and squeaky. "This staying in role is powerful stuff. I feel like a munchkin, think like one too. What do you think of my voice? Pete says it's perfect for the role."

For a moment I filled with rage, then it subsided. "Annabelle, how can I help you?"

"Shame about Leo; he seemed such a gentleman."

So that was it. Annabelle had information about Leo Warrington. I lowered my voice, heart beating hard. "What do you know about his murder?"

"Everything."

I pressed the phone hard to my ear. "Go on," I said. "I'm listening."

"Doris, I had a long chat with Mrs Symons. Do you know her? She cleans the Wainfleet Cottages, the Hidden Caves Chapel, and a ton of other places including the Silver Beach Hotel. I've no idea how a woman of her age does it, especially since she doesn't drive. Ask a busy person and all of that I suppose. Anyway, she found Leo, said he was in a bad way. Inspector Doxon told her he was in your ex-husband's room...and now your hubby is on the run. I'm so sorry for Toby. Is that his name? So sorry he is under—"

Now wasn't the time for a long story, especially about my miserable life. "Annabelle," I barked, "why did you call?" I clenched my fists.

The silence from the other end stretched out for a long while. I was about to hang up when Annabelle said, "I spoke with Mrs Lintott about things."

"I see," I said with disappointment. "So, you don't know who killed Leo Warrington?"

She ignored my question. "Today is my audition. We thought you might like to come along with me, take your mind off things. It's an open audition; you could try out as well."

"We?"

"Mrs Lintott and I." Her voice was calm, conversational as if we were chatting over breakfast in the Fiddlers Bowl Café.

"I'm sorry, Annabelle, but—" I said, then stopped when I realized my voice was getting loud. "I'm not up to it," I said in a lowered tone, unclenching my hands.

"Doris, what are you going to do today; stay in your room and mope?"

I had no plans, no idea what I'd do with the day, hadn't thought that far ahead. I glanced around the tiny apartment. Even with the sun shining through the window, it was bleak. I couldn't bear to stay trapped within these four walls all day. "Okay, I'll join you. What time does it start?"

Chapter 28

IT WAS CHAOS.

Hundreds of people spilling out of the car park and heading towards the community centre.

"Who would have thought so many people would turn up for auditions," I said as we waited in line.

"Acting is a competitive business, cutthroat at times," Annabelle replied as she glanced around and nodded with a sly eye at a group of teenage girls dressed as munchkins. "Thought I'd be late; those buses are so unreliable. I'd swear the drivers take pleasure in not stopping. I had to stand in the road!"

"You're here now, and in good time," I replied in a cheery voice. I didn't want to get into a downhill conversation about the unreliability of Skegness buses.

"Sure am." She glanced at my feet. "Why are you wearing open-toed sandals? You need gym shoes or running shoes."

"They feel comfortable." I hadn't given my footwear much thought. Now I realized she was correct; trainers would be much better.

"Doris, not everyone will make it through selection," Annabelle said in a hoarse voice. "Take those teenage girls, haven't got a chance. Our advantage is that we train every week at the community centre, and I've been in the role for days. This will be easy even if you are wearing beach shoes."

A stocky man with a barrel chest and face the colour of beetroot came out of a side door of the community centre. "Ladies and gentlemen, your attention, please." He spoke through a megaphone. "Today's response has been unprecedented, numbers extraordinary. I'd like those who wish to audition as a munchkin to line up over here. I'll take you inside in groups of about ten."

"Come on, Doris," Annabelle said, grabbing my arm and tugging me towards the side entrance. "Let's be in the first group so we can wow the director."

I scurried behind as Annabelle, like a New Year's Day sales shopper, made her way through the crowd to the barrel-chested man.

"This way, please," he said, eyes filling with anxiety at the crowd surging towards the entrance. "Inside, quick. First ten only."

"Made it!" Annabelle huffed as the man closed the door behind us. "We are in."

Our group hurried along a darkened hallway. "Leads to the backstage area," the man explained, hurrying ahead. "The deputy director will be in the audience, and he'll tell you what to do. I'm Barry."

We scurried by broken tables, old worn-out armchairs, rusty tins of paint, and boxes filled with who knew what, eventually arriving in the backstage area. Barry took several moments to jot down our names and contact details. He pinned a large number onto each of us, I was number ninety-seven. Then he raised his finger to his lips. "Please wait here while I let the director know we are ready. When you hear me clap, please file onto the stage in an orderly fashion."

We waited for several moments, the voice of Barry and the director audible.

"I need to be back at Fantasy Gardens by three thirty," a voice I assumed to be the director said.

"Got it," replied Barry. "Let's get started, then."

Suddenly, the sound of a single hand clap. As one, we tumbled onto the stage, each person trying to get ahead of the other. "Stick with me, Doris," Annabelle cried, shoving a scrawny woman, who must've been six feet tall, to the floor. "Today is our day."

"Please spread out," Barry said as he strode to the front of the stage. Again, more shoving and pushing. "Mr Hornsby, I present to you the first group of potential munchkins."

There was a long moment of silence, then from the darkened auditorium a voice called out. "Thank you, ladies and gentlemen for taking the time to come here today. Each one of you is a part of history and a Skegness winner. As you leave, be sure to pick up your voucher for a free hot dog valid at the Fantasy Gardens hot dog stand. Bring your family, friends, and anyone else for a delightful day out. The summer season begins in a few weeks. Now are you ready?"

There was an excited murmur from the gathered crowd. "This is it," whispered Annabelle. "We are thirty seconds away from the big time."

"Please let me see your interpretation of a munchkin walk." The voice came suddenly from the darkened auditorium. All at once people waddled, hopped, strolled, and hobbled in every direction. Annabelle stuck out her leg, tripping one of the teenagers.

"Follow me, Doris, and smile," Annabelle whispered. "Do what I do. We're killing it." She swayed from side to side like the pendulum of a grandfather clock and with ponderous steps waddled towards the front of the stage. Everyone else had the same idea, and there was a moment of sharp elbows as she jostled with the tall scrawny woman and pushed by the group of teenage girls. "I think the director likes me," she crowed as she tripped another teenager.

I felt ridiculous, like a hen about to lay an egg, but kept out of the pushing and shoving.

A gong sounded out.

The group continued to waddle, hop, stroll and hobble.

"I forgot to tell you," came the voice from the auditorium. "When you hear the gong, you need to stop. Part of your assessment today is your ability to adhere to instructions."

Immediately, everyone stopped, except Annabelle who used her moment in the spotlight to do a munchkin pirouette. Then she froze, as still as a block of ice, her eyes gleaming as if she sought out applause.

"Superb," came the voice again from the auditorium. "This is wonderful."

There was a slight hiss, crackle, and music played through hidden speakers. I recognized the tune as "The Amazing Fantastical History of Mr. Willy Wonka."

"Now, ladies and gentlemen, I'd like to see you disco dance, munchkin style."

Unfortunately, I was never much of a dancer. My mother forced me to take ballet lessons, but I never made much progress. The teacher referred to my attempts as a spider on a pogo stick. I haven't improved any since then. I watched with a grim fascination as Annabelle twirled across the stage. She leapt high through the air as if she were the lead dancer in the London Ballet. The teenage girls performed somersaults like circus performers. I bobbed up and down like a plunger.

"No, no, no," yelled Annabelle, twirling in little circles, all the while a plastic smile slapped across her face. "Float like a fairy, think airy not pogo stick."

The more I tried airy, the more pogo-like I became.

The music came to an abrupt halt.

Everyone stopped. I came to an embarrassing halt thirteen seconds after everyone else. My face flushed, and I knew I hadn't made the cut.

"Thank you," came the voice from the auditorium. "Our production involves a breakout scene where a group of feminist munchkins escape the confines of the chocolate factory. It's kind of like *Escape From Alcatraz* but with little people singing and dancing. Ladies and gentlemen, it is particularly important you are light on your feet. I'm looking for ladies, but we'll also need a few chaps. When I clap, I want you to sprint across the stage like gazelles chased by a hungry lion."

There was a shoving and jostling for position.

Clap!

I took off like the lioness Elsa in the movie *Born Free*. When I got to the other side, I turned to watch. Annabelle huffed and puffed like a locomotive climbing a steep hill, almost moving in slow motion. She came in dead last.

Again, the gong sounded.

"'This way, please. Thank you for your time. We'll be in touch," said the barrel-chested man.

Back in the car park Annabelle asked, "How do you think I did?" Her voice had returned to normal.

"You knocked them dead," I said and meaning it. "Where did you learn to dance like that?"

"YouTube. Everything is online these days. Pete is going to be so jealous when I get the role. He's holding out for Willy Wonka, but I think they'll use a professional actor for that."

She waved her hand. "You did pretty well yourself, especially for someone who hasn't spent the past few days living in the role as a munchkin. If they don't call you back, there's nothing to be ashamed of, Doris. You can't expect to get through on your first try." Again, she waved and strolled across the car park to the bus stop. "See you next Tuesday, and don't worry."

With no word from Toby, nothing from the police, and no job, I took her advice. "I'm not going to worry," I shouted as her bus arrived. "I'm going to take action." But I don't think she heard me over the rumble of the bus engine and the angry squawks of seagulls.

Chapter 29

I SAT IN THE MICRA staring out at the emptying car park. Heavy dark clouds rolled across the sky, and seagulls scrambled for perching space. There was a definite threat of rain, possibly a storm. Part of me wanted to mull over recent events—Toby, the murders, the lost job. That part of my psyche urged me to return to the bedsit, turn off the lights, and sulk in the darkened room.

Another part of me, the practical part, wanted to get on with life. "Sulking is easier than action," I said aloud, then added, "I've got to keep moving, and get things done." The question was, what to do? What was the next step? After a moment it hit me. "Find a new job that will scare up a few banknotes to pay the bills." I thought of Fantasy Gardens and its hot dog stand. Serving fish-and-chip-flavoured hot dogs was better than nothing.

#

ALTHOUGH THE GROUNDS were open, Fantasy Gardens was devoid of activity, only the occasional pensioner sitting on a bench eating a sandwich under the darkening sky. As

I followed the orange brick road which led to the food court,
I practised asking Mr Hornsby, casually, whether he'd filled the
hot dog stand vacancy. I hoped he wouldn't recognize me from
the audition or earlier phone call. "Chances are slim to none," I
said to motivate myself.

I strolled with purpose, confident I was at least a week
ahead of the high school crowd. Now, as I walked, I practised
what I'd learned at the community centre acting class—I was in
role as the world's greatest hot dog attendee. Head up, shoulders back, I continued to stride. The job was mine if I wanted
it—and I wanted it.

As I turned the corner that led to the food court, I saw a figure polishing the window of the hot dog stand. A cleaner getting things ready for summer season? But as I drew closer, I recognized the individual.

"Fred!" I said in astonishment, staring at the former security guard of the *Skegness Telegraph*. "What are you doing here?"

"Get lost," he spat, his eyes as small and hard as dried peas.
"I'm the hot dog cadet for the season. The job's mine. You hear
me? Mine. Now, get lost."

"Fred, you don't understand—"

"I know what happened to you at the *Skegness Telegraph*.
Lucy Baxter gave you the chop." He let out a mocking laugh.
"Jobs like this don't grow on trees in this town. You're not steal-
ing my hot dog job!"

"Fred...let me explain," I stuttered with an overpowering
sense of disappointment. I'd have made a much better hot dog
cadet. "I didn't come here to steal your job."

"Yes, you did. I've got your number, young lady. It isn't going to happen today."

I blushed, wondering why I was so easy to read. Now, I'd have to take my chances in the free for all of high school students fighting over the candy floss and giant-teddy-bear stalls.

I shuffled away, head drooped and towards the main building.

"That's right!" Fred yelled after me. "Sod off!"

The first drops of rain began as I approached the front door. It was a large arched entranceway which led into the arcade and offices at the back. Seagulls perched along the ledge, their dried, greyish black droppings splattered like graffiti over the steps.

An urgent squawk caused me to glance up. A large gull stared down with an agonized sort of grimace in its avian eyes. I was beginning to think it would keel over dead and stepped sideways as a monstrous, greyish black blob hit the ground splashing in random streaks over my open toe sandals.

"Oh bugger!"

"They say that's good luck," came a voice from behind. It sounded familiar; when I twirled around a tall, slim, rough-looking man stared back. He wore blue jeans, a rumpled white shirt, and he was almost entirely bald.

I didn't recognize him.

"Sorry?" I said, glancing around and realizing the only escape was to run by him.

His thick fingers, blackened at the tips as if he did manual work, pointed at the birds. "They call it the Skegness kiss." He raised a hand to adjust his black-rimmed glasses which were held together by white masking tape. "Getting dumped on by a seagull. It's a sign of good fortune." He jerked his head upward towards the ledge where the birds perched.

"Then judging by this state of the front door," I said, following his gaze, "this place must be the luckiest business in town."

He chuckled. "The arcade is not open for another week or so. It'll be cleaned up before tourist season."

"Oh," I said, still a little startled, and wondering whether I was in any danger. "I was hoping to get inside and speak to Mr Hornsby."

His thick fingers, blackened at the tips as if he did manual work, pointed at the birds. "They call it the Skegness kiss." He raised a hand to adjust his black-rimmed glasses which were held together by white masking tape. "Getting dumped on by a seagull. It's a sign of good fortune." He jerked his head upward towards the ledge where the birds perched.

His eyes peered through thick lenses, and his crooked teeth gave his smile a sinister appearance. "Not from around these parts, are you, love?" He moved closer, adjusting his eyeglasses and scrutinizing my face. I could smell a kind of fishy stench on his breath.

Again, I glanced around. The hot dog stand was out of sight, and there was no one else around. I drew my breath and held it for a long moment. Then I said, "No, I'm not local. Just moved into town."

"Your face is familiar, so is your voice." He leaned forward.

I stepped backwards in part to avoid the fishy odour. "Sir, we've never met."

He blinked, craned his neck forward. "Are you sure, darling?"

There was a distant rumble of thunder, and the rain came down in large drops. I prepared to run.

"Number ninety-seven!" he said before I could make up my mind. "You were at the auditions—at the community centre, this morning, right?"

He must've been one of the munchkins, I thought. "There were so many people trying out. I didn't recognize you. I'm sorry." Then I added in a friendly voice, "Do you think you got the role?"

"There's more." He rubbed his thick hand against his chin.

The fishy stench was almost unbearable. "Munchkin," I said, "How many do you think they wanted?"

He adjusted his glasses. "I know there's more."

"Sorry?" I said again, glancing around. There was a chance I could make it to the hot dog stand, but only a slim one, and I couldn't count on Fred for help. I continued to make pleasant conversation—keep 'em talking, if you will. "Do you think you made it as a munchkin?"

He frowned as his eyes scanned me like an X-ray machine. "It'll come to me in a moment."

"So, you were auditioning for another role?"

"No." The man shook his head. "That's not why I was at the community centre. I went there to look for...women."

The sound of a seagull screech caused him to look up. Two birds fought over a space on the ledge. They extended their wings, jabbing their beaks at each other like jousting knights. Eventually, one bird tumbled flapping its wings and squawking and pooping as it flew off into the distance.

"Doris Cudlow!" The man said, his lips curling into a crooked smile. "I knew I recognized your voice. You're the reporter for the *Skegness Telegraph*." He extended his hand. "I'm

Mr Doug Hornsby. I run this place. Are you here to talk about my fish-and-chip-flavoured hot dogs?"

Chapter 30

"THIS WAY," HE SAID, slipping by, reaching into his trouser pocket and pulling out a key to open the door. "It's much more comfortable in my office."

On another evening I would have made any number of excuses. But this evening there was a numbness in my mind, like the numbness I felt staring at the body in the mortuary. It was as if I was dreaming, standing there at the entrance to the building, and at any moment I might wake up. My legs moved forward under their own steam, and I followed Mr Hornsby into the darkened hall.

"Watch out, the floor's uneven in here; gotta get it fixed."

He moved with dexterity through the darkened hall. I could make out arcade games, consoles dimmed. The floor squeaked as we walked, a faint smell of dust and mould caused me to cough.

"We'll be opening for the summer season in a week or two, Mrs Symons, our cleaner, will give the place a once-over. And I'll get the repairman to give the hall a lick of paint."

He disappeared around a corner. There was a faint click, and light shone like the North Star guiding me to a small office. There was shelving along three sides and a tiny metal desk—jammed into a corner.

"This is the heart of the Hornsby empire," Mr Hornsby said, settling himself behind his desk. "Nothing fancy but good enough for Skegness."

I stood for a moment staring around the room, then picked out a plastic chair and sat down. "Thank you for inviting me in," I said, glancing around. Electronic components and mechanical contraptions crammed wooden shelves. There were no windows.

"This space doubles as our storeroom. Those are the spare parts on the shelves," Mr Hornsby said as if to answer my unasked question. "Now, do you think my flavoured hot dogs will make the first page of the *Skegness Telegraph*?"

"That would be nice, wouldn't it?"

"I've been working on the idea for years."

"Is that so?"

"The difficulty is getting the perfect balance between the fish flavour, fried potato flavour, and vinegar. Too much vinegar gives the dogs too sharp a tang. Not enough, and you're talking pease pudding without the taste. I sample every batch; wife says I smell like a fishmonger."

I couldn't wait any longer. "Mr Hornsby, I'd like to ask about—"

He raised a hand. "Please, call me Doug. Now, the plan was to test a small batch of our hot dogs at Norah Porlock's big day. She was from around these parts, you know."

I sat up in my chair. "You were at the wedding?"

"That I was. Along with most of Norah's old flames." His lips curved into a smile. "The moment the lights went off, I knew it would not be a good day for my hot dogs."

"Quite," I said, then added, "So, you were an old friend of Norah's?"

"An old admirer, at a distance, I might add. She was a bit old for me, more like a loving aunt. Anyway, I wasn't surprised she ran off."

"Really. What makes you say that?"

He glanced around the room as if making sure no one was around. "It happens more frequently than you realize—the runaway bride." Again, he glanced around, leaned forward dousing me with a waft of fishy breath. "I hear Norah's fiancé was a brute—drink, drugs, that sort of thing, and not from around these parts. Once the police capture the fiend, we'll all sleep more easily in our beds. Won't do much for poor Norah, though."

I almost sprang to Toby's defence but realized the news I was his ex-wife hadn't reached Mr Hornsby's ears yet. I held my tongue. "That's what everyone wants, to sleep easy in their beds. I think we will all feel better once this case has been resolved."

Mr Hornsby was smiling, but his eyes were in a faraway place. "When I saw Norah Porlock dressed in all white, granted it was only for a moment, a new idea struck." His eyes came into focus.

"What was the idea?" I asked, knowing it might be the missing clue.

"She looked wonderful, lost a lot of weight. It got me thinking about hot dogs. And how to make a carbohydrate-light version." He raised a finger to his lips. "Keep this to yourself. I'm experimenting with a new almond flour bun. I imagine the *Skegness Telegraph* would love to get the exclusive on that story. There must be thousands of brides-to-be who'd love to stuff their faces with hot dogs and fit into their wedding dress. I'll be offering a service that could make millions."

"Possibly," I said with little enthusiasm.

His eyes narrowed, and he leaned forward over his desk. "Okay, I get it. How much?"

"Sorry?"

"I know how these things work. I know it costs money to get on the front page of the *Skegness Telegraph*. How much do you want?"

"Mr Hornsby, I really—"

He tugged at his ear. "Doris—can I call you that?"

"Yes."

"I think you'd make a brilliant munchkin."

"Really?"

"Believe me; you have what it takes." He half closed his eyes. "Doris, I can see you in the West End, a national star in London's great theatres." His eyes snapped open. "My hot dogs are a great story, bound to go national—just like you." He folded his arms across his chest, and his lips curved into an all-knowing smile. "How much?"

I felt like a con man. "Mr Hornsby, I no longer work for the *Skegness Telegraph*."

"Are you telling me," he said slowly, "you're working my story for another newspaper—a national?"

"Not exactly."

"Mrs Cudlow," he said with exaggerated formality, "I'm a busy man; explain yourself."

The words of Mrs Lintott echoed in my mind. "Skegness is a small town; news gets around." I came clean. "Your flavoured hot dogs is an interesting story...but right now I'm...in between jobs."

He raised his thick fingers to adjust his eyeglasses. "So, you didn't come here to talk about my hot dogs."

"No."

His voice turned cold. "What do you want?"

I cleared my throat. The palms of my hands felt sweaty. "A job."

"What!"

"Maybe at your hot dog stand." Then thinking about Fred, added, "Maybe as an assistant."

He burst out laughing, slapping his hands on the metal desk like a bongo drum. "That's funny!"

"I'm serious," I said in a sober voice. "I need something to tide me over the next few months while I find my footing."

Again, he adjusted his glasses leaning forward over his desk. "That's a shame because I have a very reliable individual at the hot dog stand."

"What about the candy floss and giant-teddy-bear stalls?"

He shook his head. "I'm not ageist, but those positions require teenagers. Youngsters bring in more cash than those of us over a certain age. I wish it were different, but that's the way it is."

"Oh," I said, voice filled with a mixture of disappointment and humiliation. "That's a shame."

Mr Hornsby's eyes scanned my face as if searching for something. After a moment he said, "Listen, I have a couple of vacancies..." His voice trailed off as if he was considering.

"Yes," I said in an eager voice which didn't match the way I felt.

He touched his chin. "It's evening work and for a lady like you—"

"I'll take anything."

"It's day-to-day, depends on the weather."

"Perfect."

"Starts at nine p.m., finishes at two."

I didn't like the sound of that, but with nothing else on the table I drew deeply on my acting classes and enthused, "Sounds wonderful; what is it?"

He leaned forward and belched. A plume of moist fishy odour assaulted my nostrils. "Overnight doughnut fryer. We don't make 'em when it rains—no demand. Our first dry run is next Tuesday. Meet at the hot dog stand a little before nine, and the job is yours."

Chapter 31

WITH A MIXTURE OF RELIEF and disappointment, I entered through the glass doorway of the Golden Shores Elderly Home. Relief I now had a job even though it was as a late-night doughnut fryer. Disappointment because I was no nearer to figuring out who killed Norah Porlock or Leo Warrington. I let out a long sigh, inhaled the potpourri-scented air, and forced a smile at the receptionist.

"Back to see Reggie?" Siya asked, glancing up from the computer. "You'll find him in his usual spot"—she bobbed her chin towards the hallway—"in the sunroom."

As I walked along the hallway, a figure dressed in black rushed by. If it weren't for the long black gown and broad-brimmed hat, I would not have stopped and turned around. I did so at the exact moment the figure did the same. It was Rector Beasley.

"Doris Cudlow isn't it?" His voice was light, easy-going, friendly. "You are the talk of the town. Fancy meeting you here."

"We haven't formally met," I said, extending my hand.

He took several steps forward and took my hand. "Oh, delighted to meet you. I hope to see you in church one of these days."

It had been a while since I'd been inside a church for anything other than a wedding or funeral. More funerals than weddings lately. I half nodded and said, "You must be a busy man, running a church, and visiting the elderly."

"Don't forget the praying."

"Must take up a lot of time."

"Oh yes, it'd surprise you." He lowered his voice, looked me directly in the eyes. "Especially for your ex-husband. Toby, isn't it?"

"Thank you," I said, a crimson tide riding up my neck.

"No need. It's all part of the job. I'm also praying for justice, and that the authorities will resolve this terrible mess as speedily as possible. And I'm praying for you too." He let go of my hand, his eyes softened, lips curved into a sad smile. "It can't be easy for you, dear."

Rather than express annoyance at his prying into my business, I said, "Thank you." Those two little words often go a long way. They appeared to encourage the rector and loosened his tongue too.

"There are so many mysteries in life, so many questions unanswered." He lifted his eyes to the heavens. "I still don't understand how Norah disappeared from the chapel." He lowered his voice. "If it is any consolation to you, Mrs Cudlow, I've run over the details and by process of deduction concluded your ex-husband is innocent. I believe Inspector Doxon is barking up the wrong tree, and I will tell him so when I see him next."

His words made me light-headed, giddy. "Really? You think Toby is innocent?"

"I've no doubt about that." He was beaming and rubbing his hands together.

Now, for the first time in days, I saw a light at the end of the tunnel, felt encouraged. I wanted Toby to be guiltless, but here was someone with no skin in the game declaring his innocence. A surge of energy rushed through my body, then I thought about the hotel and Leo Warrington. "What about the discovery of—" I stopped, wondering how much he already knew.

"Leo Warrington's body in Toby's hotel room? Well, that complicates matters I suppose, but it's a mere trivial detail."

"Trivial?"

"Well, perhaps a little more than trivial," he mumbled reflectively. "Rather a large detail, one I've overlooked somewhat. I wonder if your husband has a good lawyer." He looked at me for confirmation.

My eyes looked down at the floor, and we fell into a brief silence which I broke with a question. "How did Norah seem to you at the wedding?"

Rector Beasley shook his head. "I was busy speaking with the groom when she arrived. I glanced in her direction for a moment before the lights went out."

"What did you see?"

"Nothing; it was dark."

"No, I mean before the lights went out. When you glanced at Norah, what did you see?"

He tugged at his dog collar and closed his eyes. "The same as everyone else I suppose. Norah entered the chapel in her wedding gown, looking unusually slender and tall in her shoes. Then the lights went out, and Norah had vanished. Toby was at my side the entire time. I can't see how he could have been responsible."

A tinge of excitement ran through my veins. "Rector, what do you believe happened?"

He glanced around the hallway and in a hushed voice said, "Leo Warrington."

"What about him?"

"He was Norah's ex-boyfriend, an electrician and a soul in need of, let's say, more redemption than the typical person. It doesn't take a genius to work out her disappearance involved Leo. What I can't understand is his relationship to your ex-husband, Toby. I have my ideas, but it's only speculation, and that's only one up above gossip."

The rector's idea might be the last piece of the puzzle I thought as my heart raced and mind sprinted even faster. "Gossip is malicious and degrading, but speculation... Well, that's seeking the truth isn't it, Rector Beasley?"

He thought about that for a moment. "Mrs Cudlow, I see your point. Yes...indeed. I see it clearly."

"What do you think happened?" I asked, voice rising in urgency.

He placed a friendly arm around my shoulder and leaned in close. I could smell his aftershave: musky and sweet. "It's obvious, isn't it? Leo Warrington was responsible for the electricity failure. We can agree on that, can't we?"

"Agreed."

"And I think we can also agree Norah disappeared from the chapel without a struggle."

"That seems to be a fact."

"So..." the rector said, staring at me as if it was obvious.

"Yes," I said with hesitation. "So, what?"

He tapped the side of his head with his finger. "Here is what I believe happened: Leo got in touch with Norah just before the wedding, convinced her he was her man. They planned to run away together, but after she sneaked out of the chapel something went terribly wrong."

"Go on," I said as it was all making perfect sense. "Please continue."

The rector let go of my shoulder, tilted the brim of his hat, and glanced furtively around the hallway. "They met at a rendezvous later that evening...and...well, let me skip to the next scene."

"Please do," I said, crimsoning again.

"Wracked with regret and guilt, Norah realized she'd made a big mistake." The rector touched my arm with a gentle hand. "Have you seen *Gone With The Wind*?"

"Read the book," I said, a little too sharp. I wanted the rector to hurry up and tell me his theory. "And I've seen the movie."

He glanced into my face, eyes warm and genuinely interested in helping. "Then you'll know Scarlett O'Hara marries Rhett Butler but loves Ashley Wilkes—a classic love triangle."

"I see," I said, but didn't, so I added, "and you think that—"

"Exactly," he said, interrupting as I hoped he would. "Norah still loved Toby, she had to go back, insisted her fling with Leo was their last." Waves of excitement filled his voice as he continued. "That caused Leo to erupt in a vicious rage that turned to deadly violence."

I stood in stunned silence for a moment, absorbing all he had said. Since there were no signs of a struggle, Norah had to have left the church voluntarily. Why hadn't I thought of that before? His logic was inescapable. If she went from the church under her own steam, she had to be in league with Leo Warrington. I nodded slowly. "I think you're onto something, Rector Beasley. But what about Toby?"

"He found out. Arranged to meet Leo Warrington in his hotel room...and we all know what happened next."

It all made sense.

"Two murders, two murderers," the rector said, shaking his head. "Both crimes of passion."

That Toby killed Leo Warrington didn't sit easily in my gut. For now I let it slip, knowing it was a problem I must face eventually. "Have you spoken with Inspector Doxon?"

"Oh no," the rector said, shaking his head. "These are only my thoughts, mere speculation. If what I say holds up in light of the evidence, then I'll have guessed correctly. If not, I've kept my counsel."

Chapter 32

REGGIE SLUMPED DEEP in an armchair and stared out of the window when I strolled into the sunroom. He was wearing pyjamas and didn't look up as I slipped into the chair next to him. A faint smell of stale sweat and urine alerted my subconscious. "Reggie, it's me, Doris Cudlow. How are you doing today?"

Reggie continued to stare out into the garden.

"I stopped by this afternoon to continue our conversation from earlier in the week. Do you remember?"

No answer.

"Reggie, I was at the wedding—Norah Porlock at the Hidden Caves Chapel, remember?"

Still no response.

I reached across and took his left hand. It felt cold and clammy. "Reggie, can you hear me?"

I leaned forward, peering into his eyes. They were open, but there was no light in them, no awareness. And his face was as stiff as a...

Carnival mask.

And I remembered where I'd seen this face before. In the old age homes of my childhood. Our teacher bustled us into a darkened room filled with stiff figures sitting still in wingback armchairs. They stared blankly at us children, eyes dull, devoid of sentient life, faces twisted into gruesome masks as we sang "All Things Bright and Beautiful" to the wonky piano playing of our teacher.

"Can you see me, Reggie?"

Nothing.

I wrote down my name and contact number on a slip of paper and placed it in his hand and stood up gazing into the gardens. Neatly trimmed hedges lined a large green lawn, and rose bushes not yet in bloom were everywhere. Several residents sat on benches or in wheelchairs, and others wandered leisurely along the paths that zigzagged through the flower garden.

"You here to visit Reggie?"

I spun around to see an oversized nurse. I recognized her from my last visit—the person who gave Reggie his snooze juice. "Can't get any sense out of him today."

"Darling, ain't nobody getting sense out of him. Not with all the medications the doctors have him on. Reggie the Veggie is what the residents call him now." She glanced at Reggie. "Don't they, love?"

No response.

He seemed so alive, full of energy on my last visit. I could barely believe the change. "So, you give him the snooze juice during the day as well as night?" I asked in astonishment.

The nurse chuckled. "Have you been speaking with other residents? They only give the snooze juice, as you call it, at night, helps our guests settle down. No, the doctors prescribed sedatives to calm Reggie down. Keep him from talking nonsense."

"Nonsense?"

"I told his care team it was not a good idea to take him to the Hidden Caves Chapel. But I'm just a care nurse; what do I know?"

Now I was curious. "What type of nonsense?"

The nurse placed a plump hand on her hip. "You're not a relative, are you?"

I wanted to say yes, but said, "No."

"Are you from social services?"

"I was at the wedding at the Hidden Caves Chapel. That's where I met Reggie."

She let out a heavy sigh. "I don't suppose it's a secret. Not confidential anyway, like medical records. You see, Reggie and Norah Porlock were man and wife."

She must've seen the look of astonishment on my face for she let out a slight chuckle. "The marriage didn't last long; they divorced over twenty years ago. Reggie was considerably older than her, thirty or thirty-five years older, if I remember correctly."

I did the mental arithmetic. Norah had to be in her fifties. That would make her at least ten years older than Toby. "Did you know Norah?"

"Oh yes. Norah grew up a few miles up the road. Reggie was a lady's man when he was younger, still is to some extent, when he's not on medication. She was a dumpy crossed-eyed girl with thick glasses when he swept her off her feet. But it didn't work out."

"The age gap was too large?"

She shook her head. "Reggie's roving eye."

"So that would explain why he ran down the aisle at the wedding," I said more to myself than to the nurse.

"I told them it would happen," she said, wagging a finger. "Reggie's had a bad turn since then, a really nasty turn. Can't get any sense out of him. Says his Norah wasn't at the wedding. That he ran down the aisle to warn the rector. If only they'd listened, none of this would have happened. Now the doctor's ordered he remain under sedation, and at his age, who knows for how long?"

Chapter 33

I SPENT THE REST OF the afternoon in a local coffee shop, writing in my notebook and thinking. It was getting dark when I arrived back at the bedsit. The puzzle pieces were fitting together, but there was still something missing. I took a long hot shower, hoping it would generate the solution.

It didn't.

After I'd towelled myself down and slipped into shorts and an old T-shirt, I picked up a magazine and sat on my bed. I couldn't get into it, so I paced about the room as I sometimes do when I'm feeling edgy. It helped a little—not much.

I went to the window and looked out onto the street. A woman with two children hurried along the pavement; a teenager on a bicycle weaved in the middle of the road skipping onto the pavement when a car came along. I went back to the magazine, picked it up, and the edginess was still with me. I knew what was causing it—the missing piece of the puzzle. But I couldn't put my finger on that piece just yet.

I put the magazine down, walked to the kitchen sink, drank a glass of water, and sat at the table. Quakers listen for that quiet small voice within; that's what I was going for here. The room was still, the only sound was the occasional car rumbling along the road in the street below. But the little voice within remained silent.

Then I heard them: footsteps.

Clip, clop. Clip, clop.

Steady, rhythmic, climbing the stairs. I could tell by their cadence they belonged to Mrs Lintott. I didn't want to speak to her right now. The sound stopped at my front door, and I waited for the knock.

It didn't come.

Clip, clop. Clip, clop.

The footsteps continued, climbing up the staircase.

Now I was curious. The staircase led to the dormer used these days as a storage loft. It was where Mrs Lintott kept her Christmas decorations and obsolete junk from years gone by.

I padded across my apartment to the front door and peered out. In the distance, I could see Mrs Lintott treading carefully up the stairs. Even though I could only see her back, it was clear she was carrying something with great care. They say curiosity killed the cat, but you must be curious to be a reporter.

"Follow her upstairs and see what she's doing," my inquisitive mind said aloud.

"But she might see you, then you'd be in for a long conversation, and she might bring up the question of the rent," my cautious mind replied.

My cautious mind won.

Tonight, of all nights, I wanted to be alone, think things over, and hope my subconscious mind worked on fitting together the puzzle surrounding Norah Porlock, Leo Warrington, and Toby.

I picked up the magazine, and I lost myself in an article about advances in health that would allow people to live to at least one hundred and fifty. The words mingled with the stillness of the room to create vivid pictures. As I continued to read, I was only half-conscious of the sound of Mrs Lintott coming down the stairs. The article concluded on an optimistic note—artificial organs and bionic limbs would soon allow humans to live well past two hundred years.

As I put the magazine down, I heard a sharp sound. It came from the ceiling. I sat still and listened. There it was again.

Thud. Thud. Thud.

It was as if someone was dragging a heavy object across the ceiling. For an instant, I wondered if that's how I sounded to Mr Pandy as I got ready for work in the mornings. Then I thought about my job, or rather lack of it and stood up.

Thud. Thud. Thud.

If I'd had a walking stick issued by the national health service, I might have considered banging it against the ceiling. As it was, I didn't have a walking stick, and I knew what was making the noise—Mr Felix.

I opened the door to see Mrs Lintott disappearing down the stairs. If I'd have been quicker, I would have called after her, but something held me back—the thought of conversation, I suppose. It had been quite a day, and I couldn't cope with her sympathy-laced chatter. I let out a sigh; she'd forgotten Mr Felix and locked the poor thing in the dormer by mistake, again.

I climbed the stairs muttering unladylike obscenities under my breath. At least, I thought, if I rescued and returned the oversized cat safely to its owner, I'd earn one or two brownie points. They'd come in useful given my doughnut-fryer income.

The door to the dormer swung open after a gentle tug. I waited for several moments on the landing hoping Mr Felix would dart out when he saw the light. Fat chance!

"Mr Felix," I said, stepping into the darkened room. I heard a slight scuffle in the far corner then all went silent. "I should have brought a torch," I said, fumbling for the flashlight app on my mobile phone.

The tiny light flicked on. It was bright for such a small phone and cast long eerie shadows. The boxes and containers seemed sinister under its glowing light.

"Mr Felix," I called softly, sweeping the phone's torch back and forth across the boxes and cartons as I picked my way towards the sound.

Finally, I turned the corner that led to the camp bed and the little desk.

"Hello," said a figure sitting on the edge of the camp bed and shielding their eyes with both hands from the phone flashlight.

I let out a startled scream as the phone slipped from my hand, clattering to the floor with a loud thud.

"Toby!"

"Hello, Doris, darling," Toby said, reaching out a hand towards a small lamp and turning it on. "You gave me quite a shock. I thought you were the police."

Toby rubbed his hands together, and his face was pale, eyes sunken with deep dark circles as if they'd seen too much. And he wore a threadbare tweed jacket. I remembered it as one of his favourites. On a little coffee table was an empty plate on a wooden tray with a silver domed cover at the side.

There were a thousand questions, but I asked, "What are you doing here in the dormer?"

"Hiding out until things blow over."

"But Inspector Doxon is looking for you, as are half of the Lincolnshire police force. Toby, this will not blow over." My mouth went dry. "You're wanted by the police for—"

"Yoo hoo! Toby, is everything all right in there?" called Mrs Lintott from the landing. "I thought I heard voices."

"You did," I said, stooping down to pick up my mobile phone. "What on earth is going on here?"

Mrs Lintott scurried into the room. She let out a sigh as she looked back and forth from me to Toby. Then she placed her hands on her hips. "Toby, why don't we go down to Doris's apartment and have a cup of tea. Then we can talk things over."

Chapter 34

AFTER I HAD BREWED a pot of tea, Mrs Lintott brought up a plate of sandwiches and Toby explained all he knew.

"When I returned to my hotel room, the police were outside. A hotel worker mentioned a body and my room number. That's when I decided to disappear. It wasn't a rational decision, I was in a bit of a panic, didn't know what I was doing. But I remembered you were staying at the Whispering Towers Boarding House and made my way over here." Toby spoke in a monotone as if he was reciting the words at a school nativity play. "Mrs Lintott suggested I hide out in the dormer until things sort themselves out."

"Ooh, this is so exciting," interrupted Mrs Lintott. "Imagine: Whispering Towers harbouring an outlaw—Toby's like Harrison Ford in *The Fugitive*."

"But isn't that a criminal offense or something?" I said, still trying to absorb everything.

Mrs Lintott took a gulp from her cup and nodded, eyes alight. "That's right, Doris. Maybe we'll all end up on the run!" She let out a little laugh. "Anyway, it's only for a few days until they catch the real killer. I'm sure a judge would understand that."

"So, you don't believe," I said, turning to Mrs Lintott and shielding my face from Toby, "that Toby killed Norah Porlock."

"No," she said, shaking her head.

"Or Leo Warrington?"

Again, Mrs Lintott shook her head. "No, love...and neither do you."

Toby reached out and placed a hand on my elbow. "Doris, I'm innocent," he said, and I knew then he was.

We fell into silence for several moments, then I said, "If Leo Warrington didn't kill Norah, who did?"

Toby took a gulp from his cup, said nothing at first, half closed his eyes, then spoke: "I have thought of nothing else for the past few days. The obvious candidate was Leo, but now that he's dead, I can't think of anyone else."

"What about Leo?" I pressed. "Who would want him dead?"

Mrs Lintott placed her cup down on the table with a thud. "That list is longer than your arm. A man like Leo doesn't build a successful business without crossing paths with some pretty nasty people."

"The only thing I can think of," Toby said, "was that someone in the underworld killed Norah as a warning shot to Leo. Then, when he didn't listen, they killed him as well."

If it were a professional hit, there'd be little chance of justice. Worse, Toby might take the fall. We fell into a somber silence, the only sound the occasional slurps of tea.

"Toby," I said at last, "you have to turn yourself in." A deep wave of depression washed over me. Then I added, "Eventually."

"I know. I know."

"Tell me about Norah," I said, changing the subject.

"I'll turn myself in tomorrow morning," Toby said, ignoring my question. "It's time to face the music."

"I'm sure with a good lawyer—" Mrs Lintott began.

"Norah! What did she do?" I was almost shouting. "I figured she was older than you, Toby. Short and plump, but I haven't seen a picture."

Toby stared morosely into his cup but said nothing.

"She went into accounting, like you, Toby, didn't she?" asked Mrs Lintott.

"Auditing," Toby replied in a monotone.

"Same thing, isn't it?" Mrs Lintott said, turning to give me a huge wink.

"No, it isn't! I work in corporate accounts. Norah worked as a forensic auditor."

"They are such different professions; where did you two meet?" I asked as if I was walking over broken glass.

"Norah worked for Fiddles and Tweedles, a large auditing firm on Regent Street in London. They've been around for three hundred years and work for the Inland Revenue Service." He lowered his voice to almost a whisper. "I met Norah in a bar near Piccadilly Circus."

"Fiddles and Tweedles," I said, rubbing the bridge of my nose. Suddenly there was no confusion, no vague sense that Toby might be guilty, and I knew he was innocent. And, knowing that, everything became clear. "Toby, I know you're innocent, and I think I can prove it."

"How?" Mrs Lintott and Toby said simultaneously.

I stood up, grabbed my handbag and my jacket. "There isn't time to explain, but if my hunch pays off. I'll tell you everything. I promise."

"Where are you going at this time of night?" Mrs Lintott asked, standing up.

"The *Skegness Telegraph*," I said, looking at my mobile phone clock—eleven thirty.

"How will you get in, you're not employed there anymore?" Mrs Lintott eyed me with curiosity.

"If I hurry, I'll get there as the security guards change shifts. I'll slip in unnoticed."

"Doris Cudlow!" Mrs Lintott said, standing up. "You'll get caught, for sure."

I let out a little chuckle. "I've done it before."

"Wouldn't it make more sense to contact Inspector Doxon and tell him about your suspicions?" Toby said, also rising to his feet. "I've caused enough trouble as it is. I don't want you falling foul of the law on my behalf."

But time was precious, even if Inspector Doxon took me seriously. "The inspector will take a lot of convincing. Telling him about my suspicions with no proof is a waste of time. And if I don't hurry the proof will vanish, along with your freedom."

"We're coming with you," Mrs Lintott said, and I knew by the way she folded her arms there was little point arguing.

Chapter 35

WE CLAMBERED INTO THE Micra. Mrs Lintott in the passenger seat, Toby crouched low in the back. The street was quiet at this time of night, only a few stragglers on the way back from the pub. The drive across town to the *Skegness Telegraph* office would be less than fifteen minutes, ten if the traffic lights went in our favour.

I put the key in the ignition and turned. The car wouldn't start. I tried again. The engine sputtered, and a tiny roar from the 930cc engine filled the night air. Then it cut out.

"It's like the engine's flooding or something," Toby said from the back.

"Shhh! Keep out of sight, Toby," Mrs Lintott said. "Try it again, Doris."

I prayed and turned the key. The engine turned over and purred like a contented cat. "Thank you," I said, looking to the heavens.

"Do you have enough petrol?" asked Mrs Lintott as I pulled out onto the road.

I glanced at the gauge. "No," I admitted. These days I was running the car close to empty and filling up at the last minute. "I'll stop by a gas station on the way."

On Lumley Road, I pulled into the Skeggy Stop petrol station, put in five pounds worth of petrol and slipped back into the driver's seat. All the while Toby crouched low on the back seat, occasionally peering out of the window, and Mrs Lintott looked straight ahead, with an expression I couldn't read, etched onto her face.

"Let's go," Toby hissed as I put on my seat belt and put the key in the ignition. "This place gives me the creeps."

I turned the key.

Nothing.

I tried again.

Nothing.

I looked towards the petrol station store. There was nothing particularly special about the place. It was like any other petrol station. Inside it sold magazines, fizzy drinks, sweets, crisps, and newspapers. Behind the counter was the petrol pump attendant. Only, he wasn't behind the counter, he was standing in the doorway looking out towards the pumps.

"Spot o' bother?" he asked, striding across the court. He was at the car and tapping on the driver side window before I could warn Toby. "Won't she start?"

I wound down the window as acid rose in my throat. "I've just filled up. Car won't turn over."

He stepped away, placed his hands on his hips and scratched his head. "Probably the battery. Try your lights."

I flipped on the headlights. He gave the thumbs up even though I could see they were working. Then he walked back to the driver side door. Half leaning against the car he peered inside. "Is that you, Mrs Lintott?"

Mrs Lintott half turned. "How are you doing, George?"

"Very well," he said, rubbing the back of his neck. "Is everything all right?"

"Yes," Mrs Lintott replied, turning to look straight ahead.

"It's just that—" Again he rubbed his neck, this time peering into the back seat. "It's not bingo night...and it is rather late."

Mrs Lintott turned towards George. "How is Mildred?"

"Out of the hospital and back home. The doctor says she'll need a day or two of rest. But I reckon you'll see her at bingo night next week." He leaned in through the driver side window as he spoke, craning his neck as if searching for something. "You all right back there?" he said to Toby. "Why are you crouching down?"

A car pulled into the station. And wouldn't you know it: it was a Skegness Police Station patrol car.

"Everything all right?" called the police officer from the passenger seat as the driver got out to pump petrol.

Sweat tickled my ears, and my arms were moist. I was about to answer when George said, "Yeah, her car's stalled, that's all. Think she let the gas get too low. There might be a block in the fuel line, loads of rubbish collect in the bottom of a petrol tank."

The officer on the passenger side waved an acknowledgement but made no attempt to get out of his car.

George turned back to Mrs Lintott. "What's he doing crouching down like that? I've got a good mind to—"

It was then the officer filling the tank shouted, "George, any sausage rolls in the shop?"

"Fresh out," George yelled back, straightening up. "Got a delivery due around five a.m."

"Okay, set half a dozen aside. We'll pick 'em up on the way back to the station."

George gave a little salute. "Will do."

The police officer climbed back into the vehicle and gave a sideways glance at the Micra, then the two officers sat talking, but did not leave the petrol station.

"Try it again," George said, peering into the side window, his eyes darting from me to Mrs Lintott to Toby. "If it is a bit of gunk, it will soon clear out."

I turned the ignition, resisting the temptation to glance at the parked police car. The engine burped and came to life.

"These old Micras never give up," George said with a grin. "You'll get another hundred thousand miles out of her yet."

I rolled up the window, heart still beating fast but at a slower rate. As I pulled out of the petrol station, I kept my eyes straight ahead and let out a relieved breath. I turned right onto the main road and after a moment or two glanced in my rear-view mirror. Toby leaned against the back seat peering out of the window back towards the parked police car.

"Close call," Toby said. "Doris, maybe we should go back to the boarding house. I'll hand myself in tomorrow morning."

Mrs Lintott spoke up. "Toby, you're not going down without a fight, I won't allow it. This might be your best shot to prove your innocence." Then she turned around to address him directly. "Oh my God!"

I glanced in the rear-view mirror, sucked in a breath and held it. The police patrol car headlights were on, and it turned right onto the road, directly behind us.

"They'll turn off somewhere," I said as I made my way towards the *Skegness Telegraph* building.

"Turn here! Let's take the back streets," Mrs Lintott urged in a hushed whisper.

Careful not to appear panicked, I indicated and turned left into a residential street.

The police car followed.

"Next right," said Mrs Lintott in a tight voice.

I flipped on the indicator, the only sound in the car was the tick-tick-tick as the turn light flashed. Slowly I turned the corner into a street of almost identical houses.

The police car drove straight by.

Chapter 36

IT WAS A LITTLE BEFORE midnight when we pulled into the car park of the *Skegness Telegraph*. At first, with the moon hidden behind a rushing sweep of low clouds, I'd thought the place was deserted. Then as the headlights swept across the building, a lone seagull strutted towards an empty packet; it scratched and pecked at its contents.

"Park at the far end, under that tree," whispered Mrs Lintott, pointing at a knotted oak tree whose branches arced like a broad umbrella. "The car will be out of sight there."

The branches swayed in the gusting breeze casting long streaky shadows across the tarmac. "Looks like a storm's brewing," Mrs Lintott added reflectively.

"You and Toby remain in the car," I said as I parked. "That way if I'm not back within thirty minutes you can alert the authorities."

Toby shook his head. Mrs Lintott folded her arms, but neither said a word.

I turned to Toby and half-smiled. "Darling, the key to your freedom lies in Lucy Baxter's office."

"Who is she?" he asked.

"I'll explain everything when I get back. For now, keep a watch out and call for help if I don't return soon."

I kept to the shadows as I made my way to the reception front door. A combination of fear, adrenaline, and a bladder filled with tea added urgency to my stealth. I expected to see the security guard sitting behind the desk, but from a distance, the reception area looked empty.

"This will be too easy."

I pushed the reception door. It swung open silently, and I stepped into the lobby as a clap of thunder rolled across the sky, and large drops of rain rapped on the windows.

Tattarrattat.

My eyes scanned the tiny room. I saw nothing unusual. It was as I remembered it. Then, as I stood still listening, a faint rumble became audible.

It was a gentle sound: rhythmic, soothing. I picked my way over to the security desk and peered down towards the floor. On a low camp bed, wrapped in a heavy dark blanket, the security guard slept.

Zzzzzz.

There was no break in the low rhythmic gurgle as my hand reached out and pressed the buzzer to the newsroom.

Click.

The security guard turned over, pulled the blanket over his head, but did not wake up. I smiled and half wondered if he'd still be in snoozeland when his replacement arrived at midnight. One final glance over my shoulder, and I slipped like a cat burglar into the darkened newsroom.

Briefly, the moon escaped the heavy clouds sending a white light across the cubicles. Although I'd only been employed by the *Skegness Telegraph* for a handful of days, the place seemed like home. It wasn't the tatty furniture or worn faded paint. It was that in this place I was with my people—fellow journalists. And that is what I wanted most in life, to feel like I was at home, with my people.

I had reached my old cubicle, heading to Lucy Baxter's office when serious doubts swept my mind. I hadn't thought this thing through, had acted on impulse, just like I hadn't thought through the divorce. What if I'm wrong?

The sound of a cough and shuffling feet caused me to stop dead still. Was the security guard now awake and doing his rounds?

I glanced around then scurried into the nearest cubicle. For what seemed like an eternity I crouched low, listening, my full bladder complaining—I needed the bathroom, bad. The rain clamoured against the windows, wind groaned like an angry bear, but no cough, no shuffling of feet.

After five minutes, half stooped and pausing every few steps to glance around like a nervous deer, I gingerly picked my way towards Lucy Baxter's office.

I heard it again—a low cough, and shuffling of feet. It came from behind me. I spun around, eyes straining to see into the gloom—nothing.

A sudden burst of rain kept me from hearing anything else. I sensed the person was getting closer. It wasn't a good feeling. Right here outside of Lucy Baxter's office I was in the open. I darted into the nearest cubicle, crouched low, waited. The sharp tang of stale coffee grounds and rotting banana peel from an overflowing wastebasket was so strong I felt faintly nauseous.

The shuffling grew louder. I felt as if my bladder would burst. At last, a whispered voice became audible.

"Yoo hoo, Doris. Where are you?"

"Mrs Lintott, what are you doing here?" I said as the wind continued to howl.

"Oh! You frightened me, love. It's spooky in here. Why are you crouching down there?"

"It doesn't matter," I said, standing up. "Where is Toby?"

"I'm here," he said, stepping out of a shadow. "Is that the office that contains the evidence that will prove my innocence?"

I nodded, reached my hand out and prayed the door wasn't locked.

It wasn't.

Without a word, Mrs Lintott and Toby rushed past into the room. I didn't stop them but instead glanced around to make sure the security guard wasn't up. Satisfied, I followed them into the office.

"Check the desk drawer," I said, then stopped dead in my tracks.

The room was empty. No bookshelves. No chairs. No desk. Nothing.

Chapter 37

WE STARED SILENTLY around the empty room. My legs felt numb as if I might be losing circulation in them, and my head was light as if the oxygen had been sucked from the air. Bare walls and a concrete floor were all that was left of an office that Mr Paddington had used for who knew how many years, and Lucy Baxter had now abandoned.

"Well, Doris, that's the end of it, isn't it?" Toby said, glancing from me to Mrs Lintott, his eyes glassy and shoulders hunched.

"Don't worry, love," commented Mrs Lintott. "Doris has done the best she could. Now it's time to consider alternative options."

Toby nodded. "I'll do it in the morning."

"Where is it? Where's the desk with the files?" I asked, barely hearing the others' conversation.

"They have emptied the room for redecoration by the looks of things." Toby tried to sound cheerful, but I could detect a mixture of frustration and disappointment in his voice. "Everything's gone."

I rubbed my chin. "If we can find the furniture—"

"What are you on about?" Toby barked. "It might be in a skip, or on the way to the rubbish dump or on sale in a second-hand shop or a ..." His voice dropped off.

He was right, but I didn't want to admit it. "We should still look around, might get lucky."

Toby shook his head. "Doris, we can't sneak around here all night. Come on, let's go. It's time to turn myself in."

"Don't you see? Find Lucy Baxter's new office; we'll find your freedom," I said, trying to keep hope alive.

Toby stood stiffly, glancing around the empty room, but didn't say anything.

"Listen, the *Skegness Telegraph* only rents a small portion of this building," I said, hoping he'd bite. "Lucy's office has to be around here somewhere. It will only take us a few minutes to scour the entire place."

Toby put his hands in his pockets. "Don't worry about it. I don't want you or Mrs Lintott getting thrown into a police cell. Doris, I couldn't live with myself if my actions brought trouble on you. I'll have to take my chances with a judge."

Mrs Lintott opened her mouth but closed it again.

"I'll tell you what," I said, mind racing and not about to give up. "I've got to go to the bathroom; I'm bursting, and when I get back, we can thrash things out." I tried to sound convincing as if when I came back we'd see this thing from a whole new angle.

Still nothing from Mrs Lintott or Toby.

"Okay," I said. "We all agree?"

The hard beat of rain intensified as I hurried from the room towards the bathroom. A terrifying rumble of thunder shook the building as I flipped on the light in the ladies' lavatory.

Finished, I walked towards Lucy Baxter's office, my mind racing over the floor plan of the building. If I were Lucy, I thought, where would I locate my temporary office? I was pondering this when I heard male voices: two or three at least. For a long moment I stood still in the shadows, my gaze resting on the open door of Lucy Baxter's old office.

I saw the security guard first.

"I wasn't asleep, Officers, just lying on my bed, back problems you know. They thought I was sleeping, pressed the buzzer and slipped into the newsroom. As per procedure, I called you directly."

"Excellent, sir," said a tall, thin man in police uniform. "I have to commend you on that. Too many security guards think they are Superman. Well done for following procedure."

Another police officer, a little shorter perhaps, followed at the rear. "A man and a woman you say, sir?"

The security guard half nodded. "Yes, and the woman was no spring chicken. You'd think she'd know better."

Before I could think or move, they were inside Lucy Baxter's office. For a moment, paralyzed with fear, I froze; I hadn't expected the security guard to awaken. Now Mrs Lintott and Toby were trapped in a *Skegness Telegraph* office as a result of my foolishness.

An explosive boom of thunder roared overhead, and the rain came again with vicious energy, rattling the windows with the wind howling like a hungry wolf. I made no attempt to move, just stood in the shadows listening, stomach churning—sour.

"Toby Cudlow, did you say, sir?" one of the police officers repeated.

I heard Toby answer, but his voice was too jumbled for me to pick out the words.

A few moments later Toby and Mrs Lintott left the office, flanked by the security guard and two police officers.

"Can you get on the blower to Inspector Doxon," the taller police officer said, talking into his radio. "Let him know we have Toby Cudlow in custody."

Automatically, I walked towards the exit. If Mrs Lintott was to spend the rest of the evening at the police station and Toby, who knew how long for, it was only right I did so as well. After all, I was the cause of the entire mess. I took a shortcut through the maze of cubicles ending up on the far side. Momentarily confused in the semi-darkness, I walked in the wrong direction then turned back on myself. Then I saw it—Lucy Baxter's new office.

Chapter 38

IN TRUTH, I DIDN'T see Lucy's new office as much as sense it. A door to a room along the far side wall was slightly ajar. The weak yellow light caught my attention. My head pivoted in the direction to see a small desk lamp sitting next to a heavy paperweight on Ian Paddington's old desk. How long would it take me to find what I was looking for? Not long, I reasoned as I hurried into the room. The voices of the police officers receded into the distance, and I heard the newsroom door clicked shut.

The room was a tiny space, no windows with the desk jammed at an awkward angle, and several large boxes stacked up against the wall. There was a faint smell of mould and disinfectant. My heart should've been beating fast, adrenaline pumping around my body, and all my senses on high alert, but that wasn't the case. A sense of calm washed over me. In a matter of moments I'd have the final piece of the puzzle. Toby would be proven innocent, and I'd have solid proof that would implicate the real killer.

With quiet-focused intensity, I eased into the chair at the desk and pulled open a drawer to reveal a jumble of papers. For a crazy moment I thought I was too late. But as I rifled through the documents, I saw it. A handwritten note on Fiddles and Tweedles-headed paper.

Lucy,

I still remember your teasing and bullying at school (even after all these years). Yes, I've forgiven you for making my schooldays a misery. It seems so long ago, almost like a distant nightmare. Do they seem distant to you?

It broke my heart when you poisoned Mr Tom. That cat was my only friend—I suppose that's why you killed him. I lay awake at night wondering how long the poor creature suffered, my only solace the scratch marks he left on your face.

For years I've told myself every time you looked in the mirror and saw Mr Tom's claw marks in your cheeks it was a reminder of what you had done. And I hoped it somehow changed you for the better. I was mistaken in that.

Who would have thought little, cross-eyed, plain dumpy Norah would have risen to the top of the auditing profession? Not me, but I have. Success is a strange thing.

I'm sure you are wondering why I've written to you after all these years. It is not to reminisce. I've spent the past few months going over the books of the newspapers you've managed. I need not tell you what I've found. All I ask is that for once in your life you do the right thing. You have until the end of the month to turn yourself in. That way, I won't have to share what I've discovered with your bosses or the police.

The choice is yours.

Norah.

P.S. As you know my life has turned around since school. I have met a wonderful man (in a bar of all places!) who I intend to marry—Toby Cudlow at the Hidden Caves Chapel on Saturday,

7th April. *You remember that old cave, don't you? That's where you made me watch you kill those baby rabbits. Well, that memory will be replaced by a happier one, and there's nothing you can do about it.*

I have no idea how long I sat reading the letter, but I went over it several times. The storm had ceased when I eventually placed it on the desk. I had everything I needed. Stone-faced Inspector Doxon couldn't deny or belittle me now. It was time to go to the police station.

"Found what you're looking for?" A darkened figure stood in the doorway. I couldn't see their face but recognized the voice—Lucy Baxter.

I watched stupefied as she stepped out of the shadows into the dim light of the room. A hollow queasiness filled my stomach when she turned towards me.

"You're no longer an employee of the *Skegness Telegraph*. What are you doing in my office?"

I spoke before my brain got into gear. "A little research into two murders. It's the special project we talked about."

"Trespassing, that's what they call it in law. You have no business in here."

"I know you murdered Norah Porlock." The words came out as I waved the letter and reached for my mobile phone.

The glow from the lamp fell full on Lucy's face, and I saw the look in her stone-grey eyes—murderous. "You shouldn't have read that, Doris." She stepped into the room.

"I know why you killed Norah, but I don't understand why you murdered Leo Warrington."

I watched her struggle to keep control of herself. Bright red splotches strained her cheeks. "We had a deal. I paid Leo to cut

the lights, but he got greedy when he found out I had murder
on my mind. The rat tried to blackmail me." She chuckled, her
voice cold and harsh. "So I arranged a meeting at Suite 654,
Silver Beach Hotel. The fool did not understand it was Toby's
room. He had no idea I had another murder on my mind—his.
No one blackmails Lucy Baxter."

"You killed Leo Warrington as well?"

"A sharp kung fu back fist to the temple. I doubt he felt a
thing. I know Norah didn't. And neither will you."

She lunged forward.

I leapt free of the chair and scrambled unsteadily to my
feet, snatching at the letter, jamming it into my pocket, heart
hammering fast.

"Gimme that letter, and it will be painless," she snarled.

"No," I said. "No, no, no." I hadn't planned to do it, acted
without thinking. I grabbed the paperweight and threw it with
violent force into her face. It was almost as much as a surprise
to me as it was to her.

"Arrrrgh," she yelled, pawing at her eyes, her body jerking
forward so violently that she fell into the desk. It slid backwards
toppling over the chair.

Run like Elsa the lioness, I thought, before she comes to
her senses and I'm kung fu chopped. I took off, darting around
the desk and towards the door. As I glanced over my shoulder,
Lucy steadied herself, her body twitching with fury. "I'm going
to crush your skull like a baby rabbit," she yelled.

I scrambled at full speed into the doorway.

Thud.

I hit something, wobbled, felt arms close around me but
they didn't stop my fall.

Dazed, I glanced up from the concrete floor.

Inspector Doxon's hard eyes stared back. Behind him were two other police officers and a security guard.

"Ladies," he said, staring long and cold at Lucy Baxter, "I think we'd better sort this out down at the station."

Chapter 39

THREE DAYS LATER...

The breakfast rush was over as I sat with Mrs Lintott and Toby in the Fiddlers Bowl Café. The air was heavy with the scent of fried food: bacon, mushrooms, eggs.

"Full," I said, pushing away the remains of a full English breakfast and taking a sip from a large mug of milky tea. "I couldn't eat another bite."

"Me neither," agreed Mrs Lintott.

"I'll order another round of toast," Toby said, forking bacon into his mouth and waving at the waitress. "Breakfast has so much more flavour now the accusations of murder are off my back."

I took another sip from my mug. "Thank you."

"For what?" asked Toby.

"If you hadn't told Inspector Doxon that I was still in the *Skegness Telegraph* building... Well, who knows what would've happened?"

"Don't thank me. Thank Mrs Lintott."

"Inspector Doxon's a stubborn old mule," Mrs Lintott added. "It took some convincing, but I knew his mum. I think that did the trick. In any case, if Lucy had caught you, we'd still have your mobile phone. That was pretty smart of you to turn on the recording app when you were in Lucy Baxter's office. Even without you, I think the police would have been able to send her down."

"Charming! Well, I'm still here in one piece, thank goodness."

The waitress arrived with a plate of toast. "Great," Toby said picking up a butter knife and digging in. "Doris, there's been so much going on that I never thought to ask: What was Lucy doing in the office after midnight?"

"She worked a seventy-hour week at a minimum. Most days she got in around twelve-thirty a.m. and left around four in the morning. Then she was back at the newspaper before nine!"

"If I lived like that," Mrs Lintott mumbled, picking up a piece of toast, "I'd have murderous intentions all day long!" She laughed at her own joke, as did I. Even Toby managed a chuckle.

"Everything okay," asked the waitress, clearing away the empty plates. "Would you like another pot of tea?"

"Yes, a refill would be wonderful," Toby replied. There was a sudden sadness in his eyes.

"When is Norah's funeral?" I asked, avoiding eye contact.

"I'm taking care of the arrangements," said a voice from behind.

I swivelled around to see the rector, all in black, smiling. "Just popped in for a quick cuppa. Norah was from around here. Toby's asked me to help contact her friends and relatives, and I'm happy to do that. We'll make sure she gets a proper send-off, won't we, Toby?"

Toby smiled weakly and nodded his head. "Rector, please take a seat."

"Don't mind if I do," the rector said as he eased himself into a chair. "Take the weight off my feet. It smells so good in here, and I'm feeling a little peckish."

The waitress reappeared. "Here's a fresh mug for you, Rector. The usual?"

The rector patted his stomach and grinned. "With an extra side of fried tomatoes."

For a moment the waitress hesitated, then she said, "Right you are." She turned to Toby. "The chef sends his condolences and wants to let you know your meal is on the house this morning, and that includes you, Rector Beasley."

Toby's eyes glazed over. "Thank you."

"Add an extra sausage and a couple of slices of black pudding," said the rector with a cheeky grin.

"Right you are." The waitress turned and bustled off towards the kitchen.

The rector picked up a teaspoon and tapped it against his mug. "Now, ladies and gentlemen, I'm here on semi-official business. First, I spoke with Inspector Doxon this morning, and you'll be pleased to hear Lucy Baxter has made a full confession. Hearing her own voice from Mrs Cudlow's phone did the trick. Second—"

"I still don't quite understand how she did it," interrupted Mrs Lintott.

The rector picked up his mug, took a sip, and put it down. "Well, it is all very simple—"

"Norah was never at the wedding," I interrupted.

"That's right," the rector replied, his eyes full of astonishment. "The bride at the wedding was Lucy Baxter. Remember, we only caught a brief glimpse of her before the lights went out, and even then she had the veil drawn over her face." The rector sipped from his cup. "Mrs Cudlow, how did you figure it out?"

"I didn't know at first, but then several people described Norah as short and dumpy. The woman I saw at the wedding was tall and slender. It couldn't have been the same person. When the lights went out, Lucy slipped out of the wedding dress and mingled with the guests. That's why there were no signs of a struggle or any other clues."

"That's exactly what Inspector Doxon said," the rector confirmed. "It seems Norah discovered Lucy had been stealing from Porcherie Media Corporation by firing employees but officially keeping them on the books."

"Why keep them on the books?" Mrs Lintott asked.

"To claim their salary. It appears it is a scam she has run for several years."

"Devious!" Mrs Lintott folded her arms. "And wicked with it."

"I'm afraid it is as you say," said the rector, nodding his head. "And that was the second thing I was about to tell you. With two murders and fraud on her charge sheet, Lucy Baxter will be in prison for a very long time."

Chapter 40

LATER THAT AFTERNOON I drove Toby to the train station for the 2:45 p.m. to London. I strolled through the ticket booths while Toby went to get a cup of coffee from the Railway Café. Several benches lined the deserted platform. The only sound, the gentle hum of electrical wiring and the occasional squawk of a seagull. I breathed in the salty sea air and ambled to a bench next to flower beds.

As I sat there waiting, I felt a sense of peace and contentment wash over me. I was beginning to make friends and connections in the community. Skegness wasn't London, but it was becoming home.

The mobile phone rang.

"Doris, is that you? It's Ian—Mr Paddington."

"Nice to hear from you. What are you doing these days?"

He didn't answer directly. "Shame about the *Skegness Telegraph*; such a pity..."

"What's happened?" I said with concern. "I was hoping when the dust settled, I'd get my old job back."

"Me too." There was a slight hesitation. "But Porcherie Media Corporation has decided to close it."

"When?"

"With immediate effect. Today's edition is the last. Printed newspapers in town will soon be a thing of the past. The *Skegness Telegraph* is just another nail in the coffin of a dying tradition."

"We've known for years, I guess," I said reflectively. "Newspaper circulation has done nothing but decline over my entire career. Such a shame."

"We have to move to the future, can't hang on to what was." His voice was upbeat, almost jovial.

"Thought you'd be mourning the loss."

"No, no, we are well into the twenty-first century. I'm moving with the times—everything's going digital." He lowered his voice. "Got a job as head of news media for BuzzSkeg. It's an online media outlet and covers everything bizarre and exotic about Skegness and the surrounding area. I'd love to have you work for us as a freelance reporter. Would you be interested?"

"Beats frying doughnuts."

"Eh?"

"Oh yes, and I've got an enthralling story about a bride who goes missing from the Hidden Caves Chapel."

"Wonderful!"

There was no time to celebrate because the mobile phone rang again. I glanced at the screen. It was Annabelle Brown.

"Doris, it is simply unfair!"

"Sorry, Annabelle. I don't understand what you are talking about."

"The audition! My rendition of a munchkin was perfect, wasn't it?"

"Even better than in the movies. Your voice was pitch perfect, dancing dramatic; one might even say flamboyant." I wondered whether I'd overdone it.

Annabelle didn't seem to notice. "But I didn't get selected! I've got a good mind to report the director to the police for ageism. It's hard to believe it still happens in the twenty-first century. If I had more money, I'd sue. I feel cheated...like a baby whose sweets were nicked. It's just not right. How did you do?"

"No one has called, so I guess I missed out too." Another disappointment. I swallowed it and told myself it would give me time to settle into town and get to know more people.

"Hard luck!" Annabelle said, her voice suddenly cheery. "Doris, don't be too disappointed. It was your first audition. We are treading a hard and rocky road with disappointments at every turn. See you next class."

A local train rumbled into the station. It came to a shuddering stop on the opposite platform. The ticket inspector hopped out followed by a handful of passengers, mostly tourist types. The mobile phone buzzed—a text message.

Reggie here. I'm off the medication and feeling much better—damn doctors thought I was going senile. Fortunately, the boys in blue knew better. I spoke with Inspector Doxon; he took a statement, made me feel important. Drop by and see me sometime. I'll show you around the gardens.

Using a tissue I wiped a tear of joy from my eye. Yes, I thought, I will visit you, Reggie.

"Are you all right?" Toby asked as he sat down on the bench with two carry-out cups of coffee.

"Never felt better," I said, taking a cup and sipping.

He placed an arm around my shoulder and gave me a tentative kiss. "That's good. Doris, I wanted to tell you that I still—"

The sharp, urgent ring of my mobile phone interrupted. "I'll leave it," I said, glancing at the screen and not recognizing the number. "What were you saying?"

"No, Doris. Take the call. It might be important." Toby kept his arm around my shoulder.

"Number ninety-seven?"

"Sorry?"

"Number ninety-seven, am I speaking to number ninety-seven?"

"Who is this?"

"Doris Cudlow? I'd like to speak with Doris Cudlow. This is Barry from the Charlie and the Chocolate Factory audition."

"Speaking."

"You're in! We'd like to invite you to join our production. I'll text over the details."

I clenched my fist in the air as I hung up. "Yes!"

"What is it, Doris?" Toby asked with a worried smile.

"I'm a munchkin!"

A train rumbled into our platform before I could explain.

"That's the 2:45 p.m.," Toby said, springing to his feet.

I followed him across the platform to the train door. He gave me a quick hug and climbed inside. "I'll miss you," he said with a warm wave. "Please call me."

"I will," I said, and I knew I would.

Author's Note

NOTHING MAKES ME HAPPIER than the thought of a reader finishing one of my books.

So, thank you!

If you enjoyed this story, I hope you'll leave a review at the retail website where you bought it. Reviews help readers like you discover books they will enjoy and help indie authors like me improve our stories.

Until next time,

N.C. Lewis

P.S. As an indie author, I work hard to bring you entertaining cozy mysteries as fast as I can. I've got many more books in the works, and I hope you'll come along for the ride.

Be the First to Know

Want more stories like this? Sign up for my Newsletter and be the first to know about new book releases, discounts and free books. Visit: https://www.nclewis.com/newsletter.html

ALSO BY N.C. LEWIS

If you enjoyed this story, you'll love these:
DORIS CUDLOW MYSTERIES
The Doris Cudlow mysteries are set in an English seaside town, and can be enjoyed in any order.
Deadly Chapel
Deadly Sayings
Deadly Ashes
Deadly Vestige

MAGGIE DARLING MYSTERIES
A light-hearted mystery set in a small English coastal town in the 1920s.
The Bagington Hall Mystery
The Wuthering Hollow Mystery
The Bankers Note Mystery
The Copper Moon Mystery
The Pudmore Court Mystery
The Bodham Whisper Mystery

AMY KING MYSTERIES

The Amy King mysteries are set in Austin, the capital of Texas, and can be enjoyed in any order.

Murder in the Bookstore

Murder by the Clowns

Murder through the Window

Murder in the Bullock

Murder under MoPac

Murder in Hidden Harbor

OLLIE STRATFORD MYSTERIES

The Ollie Stratford Mysteries are set in the Hill Country of Texas and offer a light-hearted glimpse of small-town life.

Texas Troubles

Creek Crisis

Bitter Bones

Magic Mumbles

Teddy Tumpin

Double Dimple

Angry Arrow

FOR AN UPDATED LIST of all books please visit: **https://www.nclewis.com/**

Printed in Great Britain
by Amazon

19261655R00108